The Billionaire Bachelor

by

Shawna Delacorte

The Billionaire Bachelor

Cover Art by *Diana Carlile*

The Wild Rose Press, Inc.
PO Box 708
Adams Basin, NY 14410-0708

Visit us at www.thewildrosepress.com

Publishing History
First Edition, 2022
Print ISBN 978-1-5092-4236-8
Digital ISBN 978-1-5092-4237-5

Published in the United States of America

**Can the beautiful socialite convince
the jaded bachelor to look beyond newspaper
headlines to the woman she truly is?**

Scott leaned back in his chair. "You really think some woman is going to dig into her purse and pull out hard cash to go with me to some unknown place? What do you do if no one bids on me?" A hint of a teasing smile tugged at the corners of his mouth. "Actually, *Ms.* Fairchild—"

"If the Ms. bothers you that much, please feel free to call me Katherine."

He cocked his head as he coolly appraised her. "Or *Kat*? Isn't that what the newspapers say?"

"If that will make you happy, then please do." Her voice came across as solicitous without actually being condescending.

"As I was saying, *Kat*"—he shot her a gleeful smirk—"isn't this closely akin to blatant sexism? Possibly even prostitution? You're wanting me to sell my *wares*, so to speak, to the highest bidder?"

Praise for Shawna Delacorte

"Shawna Delacorte's *Who's Been Sleeping In My Bed?* has an intriguing plot and forthright characters."

~*Romantic Times*

~*~

"*The Sedgwick Curse* by Shawna Delacorte is a spine tingler from the very beginning. I spent a nail biting evening racing through the pages to a wonderfully, satisfying, aha ending. Lovers of romantic intrigue and suspense will be totally captivated by *The Sedgwick Curse*."

~*CataRomance*

~*~

"*Stormbound with a Tycoon*, Shawna Delacorte's latest, sizzles with two hot characters and an interesting storyline."

~*Romantic Times*

~*~

"*Rocky Road to Romance* by Shawna Delacorte, One Scoop Or Two series from The Wild Rose Press, Inc. This book went by in a flash. I didn't take my eyes off until I finished. I didn't even notice the time pass by."

~*NetGalley*

Chapter One

"Mr. Blake, that Miss Fairchild is in the outer office. She's phoned three times this morning, and now she's here in person. I told her you couldn't see her without an appointment, but she said she'd wait—no matter how long it took."

Scott Blake reluctantly tore his gaze away from the panoramic view of San Francisco Bay out his office window. He swiveled around in his leather chair until he faced his secretary, Amelia Lambert. The expression on the prim older woman's face showed her unhappiness with him…again.

"She's a very persistent woman, Mr. Blake. I truly believe she means to remain seated there until you've spoken with her. She has one of those electronic devices and seems to be reading a book. She's obviously prepared to spend the day, if necessary."

A withering sigh of resignation escaped his lips as he picked up a letter from the corner of his desk. The letterhead belonged to the Coalition for the Prevention of Child Abuse, a worthwhile charity well respected for its efficient operation and good work. The letter was signed by Katherine Fairchild, the director of the fund-raising committee as well as chairman of the board.

"Very well, Amelia." He loosened his tie, then his nimble fingers unfastened the top button of his shirt. He had never been able to get comfortable with the restrictive dress code of the boardroom, and that morning had been the annual Blake Construction board of director's meeting. It had been five years since his father's untimely death from a massive coronary with the reins of the company passing to him. And, at the age of thirty-four, Scott still disliked suits and ties.

He had worked summers on his father's construction crews while attending the University of California at Berkeley where he graduated with a degree in environmental sciences and had planned a career in that field. As a child, he had wanted to be a forest ranger. Upon graduation, his father had talked him into remaining in the family business, allowing him to ramrod crews working outdoors in the fresh air rather than being confined to an office even though he carried the title of vice president.

"Why couldn't she just ask for a donation?" He had followed his father's long tradition of supporting various charitable organizations. "I'd be happy to write her a check. But this…" He waved the letter in the air, then swiveled his chair around until the breathtaking view of San Francisco Bay capped by the hills of Marin County once again came across his line of sight. "Let's get it over with. Send the officious Miss Fairchild in, but if she's still here after ten minutes, buzz me. And Amelia…" He turned his head toward her, flashed a mischievous grin, and winked. "Let her cool her heels out there for another fifteen minutes before you send her in."

He scanned her letter again. Even the ultrafeminine handwriting of her signature rankled him. Everyone knew the Fairchild name—old-family money, seventh-generation San Francisco that put her family's roots here during the gold rush days, the cream of society, on the boards of the most prestigious corporations and organizations. And the list went on—active in the arts, very influential in politics, major contributors to numerous charitable causes and civic projects. The newspaper constantly carried stories about Katherine Fairchild, *Kat* as her friends called her, the only granddaughter of doting patriarch RJ Fairchild. With three older brothers, she was the youngest of Edward Fairchild's four children. Her mother had died when Katherine was ten, the death cloaked in a veil of secrecy and the hint of a hushed-up suicide.

In spite of his own wealthy status, he had never thought of himself—of his family—as part of that socially elite group. Women like Katherine Fairchild irritated him. He had personal experience with them—pampered, phony, shallow, self-centered, and vain. And now this. He stared at the letter referring to a bachelor auction to raise money for the charity. She actually wanted him to stand up on stage wearing a tuxedo and posing in front of an audience and the media. Then the members of the pampered rich bid money to buy an evening with him as if bidding on confiscated items at a police auction or making a purchase at an estate sale. It seemed more akin to a cruel game played by the frivolous socially elite than a legitimate charity fund-raiser. He did not like it, not one bit.

The buzz of the intercom interrupted his thoughts. Scott rose from his chair to greet his unwelcome visitor.

The news photos of Katherine Fairchild did not do her justice. She was far more beautiful in person than in any picture. Lustrous midnight black hair, perfectly coiffed in swirls piled high on her head with just a trace

3

of coiled wisps along her cheeks, framed her finely sculpted features. He cynically wondered if plastic surgery played any part in producing that beautiful face. Intelligent, expressive turquoise eyes surrounded by the longest, darkest lashes he had ever seen. A radiant smile completed the picture. All in all, a very attractive package...*very* attractive.

Scott extended his hand as she approached his desk. "Miss Fairchild? Scott Blake. It's a pleasure to finally meet you." His smooth masculine voice resonated across the desk. "It seems we keep missing each other. What may I do for you?"

Their hands clasped. To his surprise, she returned a firm, business handshake. A soft, sexy, low-throated feminine voice floated back at him. The substance of her words, however, did not fit her tone. "It's *Ms.*, not Miss, and we've hardly been missing each other. You've been avoiding me. You didn't respond to my letter and have refused to take my six phone calls. You left me no option other than arriving unannounced and insisting on meeting with you."

He released her hand as he clenched his jaw and set his face in a hardened expression. *So—she's one of those pushy feminists, determined to prove herself the better man rather than being content to be the better woman, or more accurately, the better person.* He had been called a chauvinist on more than one occasion and did not take exception to the intended insult, although by no stretch of any thought did he consider women to be lesser than men. He believed people should be accepted on their own merits as individuals rather than proving one sex superior to the other.

"Won't you have a seat"—his voice took on an

edge of irritation—"*Ms.* Fairchild?" He took delight in her apparent annoyance with his added emphasis to the Ms.

Katherine studied him for a moment. He stood probably six feet one inch with long legs and broad shoulders. His dark blond hair with sun-bleached streaks enhanced his deep tan. His alert, green eyes seemed to take in everything. He held her gaze without looking away or seeming to be embarrassed. While not the most handsome man she had ever seen, he certainly placed very close to the top of the list. She classified him as ruggedly handsome rather than classically handsome, the only flaw being a small scar on his chin. If she were the type to rate men based purely on looks, she would give him a solid nine-and-a-half, maybe nine-and-three-quarters, out of a perfect ten.

"I'll get right to my business since I assume your time is valuable. I know mine is." She noticed the almost minuscule narrowing of his eyes and a darkening of the color. He managed to keep any further indication of his irritation hidden. "We want your participation in our charity fund-raiser the last Saturday in October. Your obligation would consist of putting together a date prize package, making yourself available at mutually agreed upon times for publicity photos and interviews, attending the auction, and going on the date with the lucky winner."

Scott leaned back in his chair. "You really think some woman is going to dig into her purse and pull out hard cash to go with me to some unknown place? What do you do if no one bids on me?" A hint of a teasing smile tugged at the corners of his mouth. "Actually, *Ms.* Fairchild—"

"If the Ms. bothers you that much, please feel free to call me Katherine."

He cocked his head as he coolly appraised her. "Or *Kat*? Isn't that what the newspapers say?"

"If that will make you happy, then please do." Her voice came across as solicitous without actually being condescending.

"As I was saying, Kat"—he shot her a gleeful smirk—"isn't this closely akin to blatant sexism? Possibly even prostitution? You're wanting me to sell my *wares*, so to speak, to the highest bidder? Isn't this the embodiment of everything you feminists so vehemently oppose?"

Katherine had encountered this attitude on many occasions. She easily fielded his intended verbal barbs. "Not at all. We certainly don't expect or advocate that sex be part of your date package. I'm sure the women involved aren't expecting to...shall we say, *sample your favors*. This is, after all, for charity." A quick rush of undaunted determination darted through her. "And a very good one, too." She couldn't hide her feelings about the plight of abused children or keep the strong emotion from seeping into her tone of voice. "We protect children who desperately need our help. I'm sorry you find that frivolous."

She remained very poised and quite unflappable, despite Scott's efforts to ruffle her composure. He watched her as she talked, her intense dedication to the cause never wavering. She had crossed her long legs, the hem of her suit skirt resting just above her knee. It went without saying that she dressed in expensive and probably custom-tailored clothes, but she also wore them well. Elegant and tasteful rather than flashy and the latest trend. He had a feeling she would look just as good in faded jeans and a sweatshirt. A sultriness surrounded her even though she made no attempt to behave in a provocative manner. She remained strictly business. Her hands rested casually in her lap, her long lacquered nails suggesting she never did any physical work.

"As to your concerns that the ladies might feel they weren't getting their money's worth, let me assure you that none of them are being hurt financially. Those bidding at the auction can afford to do so with the prime focus being the fact that the money goes to the charity, money they would probably have donated without the auction."

"If they would have donated the money anyway, then why have the auction?"

"The auction generates a huge amount of publicity, and that publicity results in even more donations for the charity while increasing the public's awareness of the problem."

The buzzing intercom intruded on their conversation. He quickly grabbed the phone. Without waiting for Amelia to say anything, he spoke into the receiver. "Not now."

He immediately returned his attention to Katherine. "Who pays for the date? Is that considered my contribution to your charity?"

"It can be if you pay from your own pocket. If the money comes from your company, then you might choose to take it from your public relations or advertising budget. The name of Blake Construction will figure prominently in all our event publicity. Or you can list it on your taxes as either a personal donation or a company donation to charity."

"So that's how one of these auctions function. What happens if I agree to this, then for some reason can't—" He allowed a bit of a grin to tug at the corners of his mouth. "—or don't want to go on this date? At what point is my obligation to this project fulfilled?"

"Fair enough question. You provide the date package to the winner, and she can take someone else."

"What does the date package need to consist of? Are there any parameters or budget requirements?" To his surprise, the idea began to intrigue him.

They talked several minutes longer about the specific applications of the money raised and the various services and programs the charity provided. She handed him a brochure outlining the financial structure of the charity, the people involved, and the services provided.

He also found himself intrigued with Katherine Fairchild. He had instantly categorized her as a rich society woman who had never done a real day's work in her life and probably never would, but the trappings of wealth and position could not hide her sincere dedication and involvement with abused children. Her face became very animated when she talked about the charity, and her eyes glowed with an unwavering devotion for her cause. He had to grudgingly admit to a growing admiration for her tenacity. Perhaps not the only thing he admired. She had great looking legs.

"Let me think about this for a couple of days. I'll call you with my answer."

"That will be fine. Other than the already specified time for the auction and its requirements, we'll do our best to schedule everything else at times convenient for you. We'll try not to interfere with your business schedule." She blatantly looked him over, making no effort to hide the sparkle in her eyes or the slight curl at the corners of her mouth. "Or your personal life."

She stood and extended her hand toward Scott. "I hope you'll accept our invitation." She flashed a dazzling smile as they shook hands. "I'm sure you'll find it interesting. And who knows, you might even have a good time."

Scott quickly came out from behind his desk. Her handshake had been business firm, yet warm and inviting. She smelled good, too, some tantalizing fragrance he could not identify. Probably one of those custom-designed perfumes that blend with the person's body chemistry. Something he saw as another trapping of the pampered rich. He watched as she walked across his office and out the door.

Amelia appeared at his office door as soon as Katherine left. "I think you should do it, Mr. Blake. It's certainly for a worthy cause. Besides, you might have a good time."

"Amelia, how many times have I asked you to call me Scott? Mr. Blake was my father." He emitted a sigh of resignation, knowing his request would be ignored. Amelia had been his father's secretary for ten years. He had inherited her along with the title of president. She was efficient and loyal, but very much *old school*.

****

Katherine Fairchild unlocked the car door and slid in behind the wheel. She had been trying to formulate her thoughts about Scott Blake as she walked from his office to the parking garage. He initially came across as arrogant, but she wondered if that might have been more of a façade than reality. He certainly had not bothered to hide any of his preconceived notions about her. He obviously considered her a pampered socialite who had nothing better to do than dabble in charity functions. The other thing that caught her attention was the aura of sensual magnetism surrounding him. She found him very attractive. And *very* desirable.

His attitude was not new to her, but coming from someone of a similar financial status, it was a bit unusual. On numerous occasions, she had encountered the same type of mindset he had projected. At first it bothered her that complete strangers decided what kind of person she was without ever having met her. After several years in the spotlight, she had become accustomed to it. At the age of twenty-nine, she had learned to be comfortable with herself, who she was, and what she had done with her life. She chuckled as she wondered if she would still be as comfortable when she turned the big three-o, an age rapidly approaching. A fleeting thought escaped from deep inside, bringing with it a brief moment of despair, then she quickly dismissed the intrusive and unwanted memory.

It had not always been that way. Growing up in the constant glare of publicity had been difficult for her as a child. Without really knowing her, the other kids had either disliked her because her family was rich and powerful or pretended to like her so they could use her. As a result, she had become withdrawn and isolated. However, all of that paled in comparison to what her mother had done to her. Even now, twenty years later, the memory occasionally intruded upon her life in spite of the fact that she had come to terms with it.

She cleared her head of the disturbing thoughts and

feelings as she drove down California Street. She had a meeting at the Hyatt Regency hotel in the Embarcadero Center. She had hoped to have enough time to grab a quick bite to eat before the next meeting, but Scott had kept her waiting. Now, she was pressed for time. The idea that he had done it on purpose poked at her consciousness. But she set the idea aside and turned her thoughts to her meeting. After leaving her car with valet parking, she hurried to one of the conference rooms on the hotel's second floor.

"Liz, I'm so sorry to keep you waiting." Katherine set down her attaché case as she quickly took in the others seated around the table. Her gracious smile included everyone as she acknowledged their presence. "Ladies and gentlemen, my apologies for my tardiness. Now"—she seated herself at the head of the table— "shall we get down to business?"

Elizabeth Torrance, executive director of the charity, returned Katherine's smile. "Don't worry about it. Jim arrived just moments before you."

Jim Dalton chuckled and good-naturedly added, "Whatever it is you want, you get my vote, Katherine. Thanks for removing the stigma from my late arrival."

Katherine laughed, too. "Jim, as much money and support as your corporation provides our cause during the course of the year, you can be tardy as often as you like." She extended a teasing smile. "And if you'd like to double your contribution next year, I'll let you be late twice as often."

"You'd better quit while you're ahead, Jim. You know you can't win with Katherine when it comes to fund-raising. She'll get your money one way or the other." Liz was a striking woman in her late forties who worked long hours making the monies raised stretch as far as possible to provide the maximum amount of help and services. She called the meeting to order, and everyone got down to the serious business, which included planning the next fund-raising campaign kicking off with the bachelor auction at the end of October.

Katherine took control of the meeting. "I've just come from talking to our last bachelor holdout, Scott Blake of Blake Construction. He's been ignoring my efforts to enlist his services. I explained the work our organization does, and he seemed to be a little more receptive to the idea. I think he'll come around."

Liz brought the others up to date on the reasons they were so eager for Scott Blake to participate in the auction. "He'll be a good one to have. There was a lot of good publicity surrounding Blake Construction following the last big earthquake. The very next day, his father had crews out inspecting every structure his company had built and scheduling repairs of any quake damage. Rumors circulated that he made repairs at no charge for senior citizens on a fixed income who didn't have earthquake insurance. When the press caught up with him at a construction site and asked about it, he refused comment. He grabbed a hard hat, climbed a ladder, and disappeared through the construction.

"Lots of people and companies gave lip service, but he actually did something while shunning the publicity. Following his father's untimely death five years ago, Scott took over the reins of the company. He's been running it with the same ethics and dedication to quality he learned from his father. That's the type of person we want to have associated with our

charity."
****

The fragrance of Katherine's perfume stayed with Scott long after she had left his office. He had very mixed feelings about her. His preconceived notions about her type—the idle rich and pampered socialite—conflicted with the reality of meeting her. As much as he wanted the two avenues of thought to coincide, they refused to become one. A nagging feeling told him his preconceived notions were going to lose.

He quickly grabbed three file folders and shoved them into his attaché case. He had a meeting and was running late. He shouldn't have wasted those fifteen minutes making her wait in the outer office. Now, he wouldn't have time to grab lunch.

The meeting with the Colgrave Corporation had been called to discuss details of the construction of their newest shopping center in San Rafael, across the Golden Gate Bridge in Marin County. They were scheduled to break ground in a few days. Blake Construction had already built four shopping centers for Colgrave, situated in various cities in the Bay area. This would be the fifth project. The two companies had a very good working relationship built on mutual trust and respect. Colgrave wanted quality, not corner cutting, and that was the only way Scott would do business. His father had built the company based on integrity and a quality product. The firm had an excellent reputation, and Scott refused to do anything that would compromise what his father had worked so hard to create.

"I hope I haven't kept you waiting, Brian." Scott extended his hand toward Brian Colgrave as he entered the room. "I was halfway to your office when I remembered we were meeting here at the Hyatt Regency."

"No problem. I was involved in an all-morning seminar, so it made sense to conduct our business here as long as I was already paying for the conference room. We have coffee, tea, and soft drinks. Could I get you something?"

"Nothing for me, thanks." Scott removed the folders from his case.

The two men discussed the final details of the construction project. After half an hour, they were joined by the project's architect, George Weddington, along with two other Colgrave employees. The meeting lasted a little over three hours and ended with everyone in agreement on the last-minute details. Scott shook hands all around and hurried down the corridor toward the elevators.

"Hold the door!" Scott shouted as the elevator doors opened, then started to close again. Someone inside pushed the Door Open button as he ran the last few feet down the hall. "Thanks for waiting."

A tantalizingly familiar fragrance wafted across his nostrils as he pushed through the elevator door. Two turquoise eyes surrounded by long, dark lashes sparkled at him, and a radiant smile met his gaze when he turned toward the other occupant of the elevator.

"It was no trouble at all." Katherine Fairchild pushed the Door Close button. "Which floor?"

"Street level." He allowed his gaze to slowly travel over her, from the top of her perfectly coiffed hair down to her high heels. She was taller than he had first realized. Without her high heels and her hair piled high, she was probably five feet seven inches. She appeared every bit as calm and composed as she had been in his office.

He flashed a mischievous grin. "Really, *Ms.* Fairchild, I told you I'd call in a couple of days with my answer. You didn't need to track me down."

"When I really want something, Mr. Blake, I don't stop until I have it."

A glint of something passed through her eyes as she returned an impish grin of her own. The look left him a little unsettled and not quite sure exactly what it meant. The elevator stopped and the doors opened.

"Ah, here we are—street level," she announced.

His gaze followed her retreating form as she walked to the valet-parking window and handed the attendant her parking stub. No doubt about it. She had great looking legs and a fluid walk difficult to ignore. He quickly caught up to her. His body brushed lightly against hers as he reached around her and handed the attendant his parking stub.

Without warning, she spun to face him. A note of hesitancy crept into her voice. "Are you busy for the next couple of hours?"

He allowed a slow grin to spread across his face as he attempted to adopt a look of innocence but without much success. "Why *Ms.* Fairchild, what in the world do you have in mind? Are we telling the valet parking to keep the cars for a while? Do I consider this a *predate date*? An *interview,* so to speak?"

Once again, the unflappable Katherine Fairchild remained calm and seemingly impervious to his purposeful sexist taunts. "Where's your sense of adventure? You'll never know unless you get into your car and follow me."

She turned toward the drive as the attendant opened her car door. After sliding into the leather seat and closing the door, she lowered the window and leveled a cool look at Scott. "Well? Are you game?"

Chapter Two

Scott slowly shook his head as he trailed Katherine's silver car east across the Oakland Bay Bridge. What in the world had possessed him to agree to follow her? He had no idea where they were going or why.

Her car came to a halt at the curb in front of an older building in a poor neighborhood in Oakland. Though worn, it appeared to be the only building on the block to have escaped the ugly defacement of graffiti. He parked behind her and cut his engine. Several tough-looking young men leaned against the surrounding buildings eyeing him and his car.

He cautiously slid out from behind the wheel and walked to the driver's side of her car. He leaned against the door, his gaze nervously flitting from one staunchly placed person to another. "Are you sure this is where you wanted to go?"

"This is exactly where I wanted to go." She stepped out of her car, seemingly without a care in the world. Her gaze darted from one doorway and alley entrance to another, taking in everyone who occupied the block. "This is Scott Blake. He's a friend of mine." Her voice rang out loud and clear as she placed her hand on his shoulder.

Scott followed her line of sight to the alley entrance. A teenaged boy sauntered toward them, his left thumb hooked in his pocket as he expertly manipulated the switchblade in his right hand. He slowly appraised Scott while keeping his distance. All the while, Katherine's hand remained on Scott's shoulder.

"Scott, this is Billy Sanchez."

"Billy." Scott gave a nod toward the young man, acknowledging the introduction.

After a long and uncomfortable pause, Billy smiled and addressed his comments to Scott. "How ya doin', man? Any friend of Kat's is okay here."

Scott shot a questioning look at her as Katherine quickly whispered, "Not now."

He followed Katherine into the building. The inside appeared neat and clean despite the old, sparse furnishings. The atmosphere presented a warm and open feel. An attractive African American woman in her late twenties sat behind the desk in the front room.

She looked up from her work. "Kat, this is a surprise. I didn't expect you until tomorrow morning." A look of relief crossed her face. "I'm sure glad to see you."

"Is something wrong?" Her gaze swept the room, seeking anything that looked out of place.

"It's Jenny…"

"Jenny? What's happened? Is she okay?" Katherine's eyes widened, a look of trepidation quickly covered her face and filled her voice.

"She's here and she's fine. It's just that she's been asking for you all day. She keeps wandering around from room to room looking for you." The woman smiled. "You know how attached she is to you, from the moment Billy brought her through the door."

Katherine's face softened as she turned toward Scott, then back to the woman. "This is Scott Blake. Scott"—she gestured toward the woman—"this is Cheryl Johnston. Cheryl runs our Oakland center."

Scott held out his hand. "It's a pleasure to meet you, Cheryl."

She returned his handshake from behind her desk as she smiled warmly. "Same here." She indicated the stacks of paperwork in front of her. "If you'll pardon me, I'm up to my, uh, *posterior* in an ever-growing backlog. I'd better get back to work before the boss catches me goofing off." She shot a quick grin toward Katherine.

"Hopefully, we'll have you some help soon. We allocated the funds at today's board meeting. Now, it's just a matter of finding the right person. This isn't exactly a prime location. Lots of people are uneasy about coming into this neighborhood."

A small voice floated through the room. "Kat! Kat!" Little feet padded across the floor as an angelic, golden-haired tyke of about three ran to her.

Katherine Fairchild kicked off her high heels, dropped to her knees, and held open her arms to welcome the little girl. "Jenny, my little darling." She drew the child quickly into her embrace and held her tightly as she rocked her back and forth. Then she placed a loving kiss on the child's cheek. "Have you been a good girl today?"

"Yes, Kat."

The little girl snuggled in Katherine's arms, her small hand closing around the soft silk of Katherine's blouse, tugging and pulling at it in her excitement. One final tug was too much for the thread holding the top button. It broke and the button popped off, allowing the blouse to gap. Katherine seemed not to be aware of the missing button. Scott, however, could not help noticing the delightful fullness of creamy skin that disappeared into the delicate lace cup of her bra.

Katherine lifted the squirming little girl in her arms as she rose to her feet. She swung around so they were both facing Scott. "Jenny, this is Scott. He's a friend of mine. Can you say hello to him?"

He smiled at the little girl. "Hello, Jenny."

Wariness crept into the child's eyes. She pulled as far away from him as she could while wrapping her arms tightly around Katherine's neck. She turned her head away, burying her face in Katherine's shoulder.

Surprise and confusion hit Scott. "What did I do wrong?"

Katherine continued to hold Jenny, rocking the child gently in her comforting embrace. "It's okay, Jenny. Scott is my friend. He won't hurt you." The little girl's head remained buried, her face hidden from sight. "Won't you please say hello to Scott? I'm sure he'd like to see your pretty smile."

Jenny's blonde curls bounced as she shook her head, keeping her face buried.

Katherine's voice continued to drift softly across the child's presence. "Please, Jenny, would you say hello to Scott? For me?"

The little girl slowly raised her head and tentatively glanced at him. Again, he offered the child a warm smile and reached his hand out toward her.

Tears welled in Jenny's eyes, and she started to cry. Scott quickly withdrew his hand and stepped back. Katherine held the little girl tightly as Jenny buried her face against Katherine's suit jacket, her tears soaking the fabric.

Katherine carried the crying child from the room. Turning toward Cheryl, he seated himself on the corner of her desk. "What happened? Why did she cry? I'm not accustomed to being around children. Did I do something wrong that scared her?"

"It's a very sad set of circumstances." Compassion and frustration filled Cheryl's voice. "The child's name is Jenny Hillerman. Her mother's current boyfriend, in a long string of many, beat Jenny. Her mother did nothing to stop it. Didn't want to take a chance on doing anything that might cost her the services of her current superstud."

Scott couldn't hide his surprise at her choice of words.

"These are the streets, Scott. That was the cleaned-up version for your benefit. There's no room here for the proper words used by polite society."

"How did you get her?"

"Billy found her about six o'clock one morning, cold, bruised, and huddled in the doorway of the apartment building where she lived. It didn't take long for Billy to determine that the mother and boyfriend had skipped out, abandoning Jenny. He brought her here. She's still a little wary of men, but she's coming out of it. Fortunately, her mother had only been with the current boyfriend for a couple of months, so there wasn't a long history of physical abuse to try to overcome."

Scott liked Cheryl. She appeared to have things well in hand and, as he had observed of Katherine Fairchild, seemed to be truly dedicated to the work of the charity.

"Are you here full time? I mean, as an employee rather than a volunteer?"

"That's me. File clerk, receptionist, chief bottle washer, and a master's degree in psychology. It was Kat's idea to hire someone with a degree in child psychology rather than the normal situation of someone with a degree in sociology, social services, or business administration. She felt that even if these kids are here only for a few weeks, it's to their advantage to start some type of psychological counseling as soon as they arrive.

"We try to be more than just a temporary holding facility for these kids until they are returned to their own homes or placed in foster homes. The really young ones, like Jenny, have a good chance of coming through things without permanent emotional scars if we can get them help right away. The length of time they've been exposed to the abuse is shorter, therefore the amount of damage we have to undo is less. In Jenny's case, it's much less because it wasn't her mother who did the beating. As I said, it was a very recent situation with the mother's current boyfriend.

"We have to let these kids know that someone cares about them. Kat is a tiger on the subject. These kids need to know they're not alone, that what has happened to them is absolutely not their fault rather than it being the result of something they did wrong." Cheryl glanced in the direction that Katherine had taken the little girl. "Jenny is going to be just fine. She couldn't ask for anyone better to take care of her than Kat."

A thought had been formulating in the back of

Scott's mind, something that would never have occurred to him had he not been at the center. "Kat said something about getting you some help. Exactly what type of help are you looking for?"

"I'll take any type of help I can get. Mostly I need someone who's organized, good with paperwork and people, who is able to deal with pressure and stress. Any time you do something connected with any government agency, there's twice the paperwork. I guess what I really need is someone who can function as my administrative assistant. That's a very fancy title that means doing a little bit of everything and not having anyone except me appreciate it. I need someone who can take part of this load"—she indicated the stacks of file folders on her desk—"off my hands and let me spend more time working with the kids." She cocked her head and gave Scott a questioning look. "Do you know someone who might fit our needs?"

Scott smiled at Cheryl and gave her a quick wink as he stood up. "I just might."

"I think we're okay for now." Katherine's voice came from the rear hallway as she entered the room. "Jenny's asleep." She turned her attention to Scott. "I'm sorry about the interruption. She's still uncertain about her surroundings and wary of new people. I thought she might take to you if she saw you with me…" Sadness clouded her features. "I guess it's just going to take more time."

Her expression brightened. "Come, let me give you a tour." She grabbed his hand and pulled him across the room. "I want you to see what our work is all about."

Even after she had released his hand, the tingling warmth of her touch lingered in his consciousness. For half an hour, she showed him around the building. She explained how this particular center functioned between the reality and needs of the people in the community, the bureaucracy of government agencies, and the courts. The center was licensed to house up to ten children at a time as a temporary facility, but some remained at the center for many months before their disposition could be determined. The center employed six people in addition to Cheryl.

"How does Billy fit into this? Cheryl said he brought Jenny to the center."

"It's Billy Sanchez's neighborhood. He runs things down here. I first met him four years ago. This center had been open for three months and, like every other building in the neighborhood, was subject to constant vandalism. One day a tough, defiant thirteen-year-old street kid burst through the front door pulling a dirty, bedraggled little eight-year-old girl behind him. He looked around and demanded to know who was in charge. Taking a deep breath and trying not to show my uneasiness bordering on fear, I told him I was in charge.

"He looked me over, jerked his head toward the front door, and asked if the fancy wheels out front belonged to me. I told him they did. He just sneered, told me I obviously couldn't know anything about anything and started to walk away. The little girl he had in tow looked so frightened. I just couldn't let him walk out with her, not until I knew what was going on. I reached out, grabbed his arm, and pulled him to a halt."

"It would seem to me, *Ms.* Fairchild, that you did a very foolish thing."

"That's the conclusion I came to when he wheeled around and glared pure venom at me. He jerked his arm out of my grasp and told me never to touch him again if I knew what was good for me. I held his gaze, determined not to look away or flinch. After what seemed like an eternity, he began to soften.

"The little girl with him was his sister. His story was my first experience in dealing directly with the horror of the everyday lives of the people we're trying to help. Up until then, I had only seen the fund-raising side—using my contacts to solicit donations, attending meetings, organizing events..." She paused long enough to shoot him a knowing look. "...all the things you assume to be my sole function in life. You see, Scott, it's been a constant uphill battle to combat people's preconceived notions about me. It seems everyone wants to believe the worst." She expelled a sigh of resignation. "I suppose it's human nature, but that doesn't make it any easier to live with."

A twinge of guilt assaulted him, quickly followed by embarrassment as heat flushed across his cheeks. He wanted to say something in defense of his attitude and thoughts, but he couldn't think of anything. She had nailed him but good. He caught the fleeting look of anguish in her eyes before she continued.

"Billy's father had deserted the family shortly after his sister was born. His mother became a junkie. As soon as she was hooked, her pusher turned her to prostitution. He added her to his stable of women, all hooked on junk. Billy dropped out of school in seventh grade and spent most of his time on the streets, picking up odd jobs where he could and stealing when necessary. His prime objective was to protect his sister. He had long since written off his mother. He came home one day and found his mother totally out of it and her *customer* trying to rape his sister."

Scott physically flinched. "My God…"

"Being a man of action rather than words, Billy grabbed the first thing he could find, bashed the would-be attacker over the head with a table lamp, grabbed his sister, and took off. He wasn't sure where to go. He could always find a place to sleep on the streets, but he knew his sister needed somewhere safe. There was no way he'd ever go to the authorities. So he screwed up his courage and came here.

"We gave her a bath, clean clothes, a hot meal, had a doctor check her, then a warm bed. He came back the next day to see how she was. When he found out everything was okay, he gave us his stamp of approval. From that day forward, we haven't had any problems. Billy's boys watch over the center and carefully screen all strangers who come into the neighborhood."

"Yes, I noticed them giving me the serious once-over."

"That's why I immediately told them who you were. Otherwise, you probably wouldn't have a car when you tried to leave."

Scott smiled. "Thanks for the help. I appreciate it and so does my insurance company." His manner turned serious. "What happened with Billy's sister?"

"We found a nice foster home for her. At first, the courts gave us a lot of trouble. The problem was quickly but tragically resolved. The next month, the mother died of an overdose."

"I must say, Ms. Fairchild—"

"I see you finally dropped the added emphasis to the Ms., but do you think you could drop the Ms. entirely? I feel we're beyond that, don't you?"

Her smile dazzled him as did the sparkle in her turquoise eyes. He held her gaze for a long moment, his pulse rate increasing ever so slightly. "Yes, I believe you're right."

After finishing the tour, Scott drove back across the Oakland Bay Bridge, his mind filled with the sights and words he had absorbed over the previous two hours. It had really been an eye-opening education. If Katherine Fairchild felt his participation in a bachelor auction would help the cause, then it would certainly be petty of him to refuse simply because he found it inconvenient or because it made him feel uncomfortable. He would call her first thing in the morning.

He called Amelia from his car and told her he would not be returning to the office. He drove through town and continued north across the Golden Gate Bridge to the Tiburon exit. Skirting the bay, he turned onto a winding side road and climbed the hill until he came to the circular drive in front of the older house resting high on the hill overlooking San Francisco bay. The spectacular view included Angel Island, Alcatraz, the towers of the Golden Gate Bridge, and the skyline of San Francisco.

Scott had always loved this view. It pleased him that his mother had decided to keep the house after his father died. At first, she had been afraid there would be too many memories for her to handle. She had finally realized they were good memories of warm and loving times. Memories she didn't want to lose.

"Mom? Hello, is anyone home?" Receiving no answer, he wandered through the house toward the backyard. Looking through the back screen door, he spotted his mother working in her garden. He watched her for a moment. For a woman fifty-six years old, she had a remarkably youthful appearance and possessed the energy of someone at least fifteen years younger.

"You know, Mom—"

Her startled face looked up at the intrusion of the male voice. "Scott! What a surprise."

"You're really much too vibrant a woman to spend your time and energy just working in the yard. How would you like something really worthwhile to do?"

"Uh-oh, what are you trying to get me involved in now? You know how much I love my garden."

He noted the suspicious look in her eyes and offered her his most charming smile. "Let's go out to dinner. We haven't done that for quite a while."

"I see. 'Welcome to my web,' said the spider to the fly." His mother returned his smile as she gathered her things and walked across the yard. "Give me a few minutes to clean up and change clothes, then I'll be happy to endure yet another of your many plans for getting me out of the house more often."

"You're going to like this one." He pumped all the enthusiasm he could muster into his voice. "It's right up your alley."

Scott wandered around the living room while waiting for his mother. He picked up framed photographs, looked at them, and set them down. He, too, had many good memories of the house, memories of a happy childhood spent with loving parents. A father never too busy or too tired to go out in the yard and play catch with a little boy, even though he worked long hours. A mother who always had time to read him a bedtime story, even though her days were taken up by her job as a schoolteacher and her evenings spent taking care of the house and her family.

His mind drifted to family camping trips in the mountains, especially Yosemite National Park, located only about two-hundred-fifty miles away. Camping trips that had instilled in him his love of nature and concern for the environment. His father had taught him how to identify plants and birds, how to recognize geologic formations, and what they meant. How to hike a trail without making a negative impact on the wilderness. He thought of family weekend outings and what his mother had always referred to as *our Sunday afternoon drive*. Always new things to see—the zoo, the aquarium, several different museums. Always something to stimulate his curiosity.

A pang stabbed at him as he thought about how ideal his childhood had been, especially compared with Billy and his sister—and little Jenny Hillerman. He felt ashamed that he had ignored Katherine Fairchild's letter and phone calls without even bothering to find out what they were about, basing his actions solely on his beliefs about a woman he assumed to be nothing more than a pampered socialite.

His mother interrupted his thoughts.

"I guess I'm ready." She gave him a knowing smile. "I don't suppose you'd like to tell me what this is all about and get it over with before we eat, would you?"

"No, I don't suppose I would." He held the front door open for her as he tried to suppress a little grin.

****

Katherine Fairchild turned into the long drive leading to the stunning Victorian mansion in the Pacific Heights area of San Francisco. It had been a couple of weeks since she had visited her grandfather. He had purchased the mansion fifty years ago and subsequently acquired the properties on each side of his house, then cleared the dwellings and redid the landscaping to give him more privacy and land surrounding his house. He had been confined to a wheelchair for almost five years and was not in the best of health. She did not like going this long between visits, but the plans for the charity auction and the upcoming fund-raising campaign had kept her very busy. She had not spent as much time at the Oakland center as she would have liked, either.

"Grandpa, how are you feeling?" Katherine knelt next to his wheelchair, giving him a big hug and kiss on the cheek. "You're looking good."

Her grandfather, RJ Fairchild, leveled a stern look at his granddaughter. "Katherine, how many times do I need to tell you that *grandpa* is not a proper term? The word you are looking for is grandfather."

She refused to be put off by his scolding and gruff attitude. From the time she was a little girl, she had been able to wrap the formidable RJ Fairchild around her finger. She gave him a knowing smile and another kiss on the cheek. "I don't know, Grandpa. I guess you'll just have to keep telling me until I get it right."

His gnarled old hand patted her hand as he gave her a loving look. "Don't you dare let anyone else hear you call me that. How can I maintain a position of respect and authority when my own granddaughter—"

"Stop being an old fuddy-duddy. You can pull that stuff on other people but not on me. You know you like it when I call you *Grandpa*." She stood up and pushed his wheelchair into the garden room at the back of the house, his favorite place in the large mansion. "I met a very interesting man today, Grandpa."

The old man's attention immediately perked up. "Did you? Does this mean I might at long last hear the patter of little feet? Be able to look at my great-grandchild before I die?"

"Stop being so dramatic," she teased. "You're a long way from dying, and you have lots of great-grandchildren. All three of my brothers have provided you with great-grandchildren, and Uncle Charlie's two sons have given you great-great-grandchildren. I'll bet you can't even remember the names of all your great-grandchildren."

"It's not the same, Katherine. You are the only girl. I have no daughters, and you are my only granddaughter. You should be providing me with great-grandchildren."

"Really, Grandpa. It's the twenty-first century. Get with the times. Women have a place in the world other than cleaning house and making babies." She poured them each a glass of wine from the bar cart and sat next to him. Everyone else found him irascible and intimidating. No one dared talk to him the way Katherine did. She dearly loved the old man, and he clearly doted on her.

"I am too old to *get with the times*, as you say. Now, tell me about this young man. What does he do, and where did you meet him? I want to know all about his background. We can't have another situation like that—"

"Please, Grandpa." Her sharp words cut him off before he could finish his sentence. She knew exactly what he was going to say—another situation like her impetuous and ill-fated marriage to Jerry during her

31

sophomore year of college. A situation that had cost the family five hundred thousand dollars, left her with deep emotional scars, and definite opinions about marriage. It had been yet another childhood legacy left to her by her mother, a burning desire to have someone love her. It had taken a long time for the wounds to heal, for her to rebuild her self-esteem and get on with her life. "All I said was I had met an interesting man. I didn't say anything about a potential husband."

"Katherine—" He reached out and took her hand in his. "—you're almost thirty years old. Don't you think it's time you married and started a family?"

She wrinkled a frown across her brow. A faraway, haunted sensation darted quickly through her consciousness. Even now, an occasional memory from the past tried to reestablish itself. "I'm not looking for another husband. I've already had one, remember?" She offered him her best smile. "Now, can we drop the subject of husbands and marriage?"

He patted her hand and smiled. "All right. Now, tell me about this interesting man you met."

Katherine remained with her grandfather for most of the evening. She told him about her latest activities with the charity, the current status of the bachelor auction, how Scott fit in, the newest crisis at the Oakland center, and little Jenny Hillerman. "Grandpa, it just tears my heart out. You should have seen her when I tried to get her to say hello to Scott." She allowed a slight smile to turn the corners of her mouth. "And you should have seen the scared look on Scott's face when she started to cry."

"And which one of them was responsible for that?" He pointed to the missing button from her blouse.

She looked down, noticing the loss of the button for the first time. "Oh!" She shot him a sly grin. "If it had been Scott, I certainly wouldn't be telling you about it."

The hour grew late before Katherine left her grandfather's house. They had talked the entire time, just the two of them, and enjoyed dinner together. Upon departing, she had promised not to wait so long until her next visit.

Katherine drove straight home from her grandfather's house. She pulled into the two-car garage on the ground level of her three-story house in the Marina district. Ignoring the small elevator, she climbed the stairs to the third floor, her private domain shut off from the rest of the world. The entire third level consisted of her bedroom suite with bathroom, an office, and a large deck with a breathtaking view of the bay with the green hills of Marin County in the background.

She quickly kicked off her high heels and shed her clothes, opting for a pair of jeans and a T-shirt. The thick carpeting felt good on her bare feet as she walked into the bathroom. She washed off her makeup, brushed out her long hair, and pulled it back into a ponytail. Even though it was late, she still had about two hours of paperwork to do before she could go to bed. Reluctantly, she picked up her briefcase from where she had dropped it on her antique, four-poster bed and carried it into her office.

She sat at her desk, but work eluded her. Her mind kept drifting to Scott Blake. Telling her grandfather she had met an *interesting man* represented an understatement of the most monumental proportions.

When she had told Scott she usually got what she set her sights on, she had been deadly serious. However, she had failed to mention that she wanted Scott and not just for the charity auction, either. The moment she met him face-to-face in his office and felt the warmth of his handshake, heard his smooth, masculine voice, and saw his dazzling smile, she knew he was someone special. She didn't know exactly how, at least not yet, but she would make him see the real Katherine Fairchild. Not the one whose name and picture constantly adorned the society pages and about whom he obviously had very definite preconceived ideas.

Running into him at the Hyatt Regency had been a real stroke of luck. Or perhaps it had been fate. She saw how impressed he was with the tour of the Oakland center and the work they did. No doubt in her mind he would accept her invitation to participate in the auction. She took a few extra moments to speculate on what type of date package he would put together. Perhaps an elegant dinner followed by the theater.

An image of Scott Blake danced across her closed eyelids—very tan, dark blond hair, intense green eyes, and about a thousand perfect white teeth that showed whenever he flashed his dazzling smile. Her breathing quickened ever so slightly as she recalled the way he slowly looked her over in the elevator at the Hyatt.

"You don't know it yet, Scott Blake, but you're mine.   All   mine."

Chapter Three

It had been an hour since Scott left his mother's house following dinner. He opened the sliding glass door and stepped onto the deck of his house, looking out over the bay. He, too, lived in Tiburon where he had grown up. His house sat right on the water, very close to the downtown village area and the yacht club where he kept his sailboat. The damp night breeze caused a slight shiver to rush across the surface of his skin.

To his surprise, his mother had seemed fairly receptive to his suggestion about working at the Oakland center. She had promised to go with him the next afternoon to meet with Cheryl. He would call Cheryl in the morning to set up the appointment.

Then he would call Katherine Fairchild and tell her of his decision to participate in the bachelor auction. Funny, when he told his mother about the auction and his initial reaction to it, she told him he ought to do it, that it might be fun. That made three women in one day telling him the same thing.

Katherine's perfume, or rather his memory of the fragrance, still tickled his senses. A spicy, sexy scent without being overpowering. He still felt the warmth of her hand clasping his. When he closed his eyes, a vividly real image of her face appeared before him— her exquisite turquoise eyes, her jet-black hair framing the creamy, smooth texture of her skin.

She had him confused. Aggressive feminists held no interest for him. And rich, pampered, aggressive feminists who lived on the society pages of the newspaper and online in various social media came in at the very bottom of his list. Yesterday, before he had met her, he knew everything about Katherine Fairchild he needed or wanted to know. Today, he realized he knew nothing about her and wanted to know everything.

As soon as Scott arrived at his office the next morning, he called Cheryl Johnston and set up an appointment for two o'clock that afternoon for his mother to meet with her. Cheryl seemed very pleased, especially when she heard his mother's qualifications. Next, he placed a call to Katherine at the number she had given him. The number belonged to the business office of the charity rather than her personal number. He spoke to Liz Torrance and told her of his decision to participate in the auction.

Katherine represented everything he disliked in women. She also constantly invaded his thoughts. He put aside that annoyance and turned his attention to the workload on his desk. The morning proved to be busy. Time passed quickly as it approached the lunch hour.

"Mrs. Blake, what a pleasure to see you again." Even from inside his office, he could hear Amelia's genuine affection for his mother.

"Hello, Amelia. It's nice to see you again, too. Is Scott in? I'm a little early for our meeting, but I thought we might be able to have lunch together."

"He's on the phone at the moment. He'll be right with you."

"Uh-oh, when the two of you get together, all of a

sudden I'm twelve years old again," Scott interrupted their conversation.

"I know I'm a little early. I thought we might have lunch together." Lynn casually brushed some stray locks from his forehead as she spoke. "If not, I have some shopping—" She turned her attention to Amelia, a thought suddenly occurring to her. "Why don't you and I have lunch together if you don't already have plans? We haven't done that in a long time. It'll be nice to have a chance for some uninterrupted conversation." She shot a sly grin in Scott's direction, then turned back to Amelia. "You can fill me in on what my son has been up to lately."

"Well…" Scott chuckled. "…that was a quick about-face. You invite me to lunch and tell me I'm dismissed, all in one sentence."

"Would you like to go with us, dear?" Lynn gave him her very best impression of innocence.

"Not a chance. One of you would tuck a napkin under my chin and the other would cut up my food— food you ordered from the children's menu." Scott glanced at his watch. "Take two hours. I'll see you back here at one-thirty."

His mother patted him on the cheek. "You're a good boy. Your mother raised you right."

Scott rolled his eyes upward as he slowly shook his head. In a pleading tone, he asked, "What did I do to deserve this?"

Amelia's face held a look of uncertainty. "Two hours for lunch, Mr. Blake? Are you sure that's okay?"

"Amelia, I'm the boss. At least that's what it says on paper. I'm allowed to make that type of executive decision. Now, the two of you, get out of here and enjoy yourselves." He escorted the women out of Amelia's office and to the receptionist's desk. "I'll see you later."

After lunch, Scott drove his mother to the charity's Oakland center. He opened the car door for her while looking around the street, checking out the various boys *on duty*. He didn't see Billy anywhere and immediately wondered if his car would be safe. He grabbed the paper bag from the back seat and tucked it under his arm. After he gave another quick glance around the street, they went inside the building.

"Cheryl, this is my mother, Lynn Blake. Mom, this is Cheryl Johnston. She's in charge of the Oakland operation and is in need of some first-class help in exchange for a third-class salary."

Cheryl shot him a quick look, then turned her attention to Lynn as she extended her hand and a welcoming smile. "It's a pleasure to meet you, Lynn. What Scott says is true, although I wouldn't have phrased it quite that way."

She took his mom on a tour of the facility, leaving Scott to fend for himself. His sharp gaze quickly scanned the room, then came to rest on a tiny face with two big brown eyes peeking around the corner from the hallway, a face surrounded by a mass of blonde curls.

He immediately sat on the floor so he wouldn't tower over the little girl. He reached into the paper bag and withdrew the teddy bear he had purchased while Lynn and Amelia were at lunch. He held it out toward the child. Using his most sincere smile and a soft voice, he called to her, "Hi, Jenny. Remember me? My name's Scott. I'm Kat's friend. I'd like to be your friend, too. I brought you a present. Would you please come over here and say hi to me? I'd like to see you smile. Kat says you have a pretty smile. Would you show me?"

He waited, remaining very still as Jenny edged her way around the corner from the hallway into the main room. He continued to talk to her, his voice soft and soothing while being very careful not to make any sudden moves or gestures. She slowly made her way across the room toward him, pausing to hide behind each piece of furniture she encountered before continuing.

****

Katherine pulled up in front of the center, noting Scott's car parked at the curb. Cheryl had called her right after she talked to him about his mother. Liz had called her right after she talked to him about the auction. Katherine smiled as she closed the car door and turned toward the building. No doubt he would get a big head if he had any idea how many people had awaited any word from him. Everything seemed to be working out perfectly, even sooner than she had hoped.

Giggles and screams of delight greeted her as she opened the front door. Scott sat cross-legged in the middle of the floor with Jenny clutching the teddy bear and squirming in his arms as he tickled her. Tears welled in her eyes as she watched them laughing and playing together. If there had been any doubt in her mind about Scott Blake's character, it had just been banished forever.

"Kat…Kat." Jenny wiggled her way out of his grasp and ran to her.

"Hi, Jenny. Have you and Scott been having a good time together?" She wrapped the giggling little girl in her arms and picked her up.

"Scott tickled me. He made funny faces."

"What do you have here?" Katherine indicated the teddy bear.

"That's Teddy. Scott gave me Teddy."

"That was nice of Scott. Did you tell him thank you?" She flashed him a grin as he quickly rose to his feet. He tried to hide his face from her but not fast enough. No question in Katherine's mind. Being caught playing with Jenny embarrassed him.

"Well, uh, my mother and Cheryl are, uh—" Scott motioned in the direction they had gone. "They're touring." He couldn't make eye contact with Katherine and desperately wanted to change the subject as quickly as possible. "I called the office this morning and talked to someone named Liz Torrance. I told her I had decided to participate in your auction."

As Scott talked, he became aware of what she had chosen to wear—designer jeans and shirt, Italian flat-heeled shoes, very little makeup, and her hair done in a French braid. The fashionably perfect socialite he had met yesterday seemed to have disappeared...somewhat. The clothes still had a designer label, but they were casual rather than something out of this year's catalog of what the stylish, pampered rich should be wearing. What surprised him most was her almost complete lack of makeup and the simple styling of her hair. For the first time, he accepted the truth of her flawless skin, that a naturally beautiful and desirable woman stood before him.

He, too, had dressed in a manner more conducive to comfort. Yesterday, he had a Board of Directors meeting in the morning and a business meeting with Brian Colgrave that afternoon, which had called for a suit and tie. Today, he'd dressed in a manner more befitting his personality—jeans and a pull-over shirt.

"I'm pleased you decided to accept." She flashed a radiant smile. "Now, I'm sure the event will be a rousing success. Have you given any thought to your date package?"

"Not yet. It was just this morning that I made the decision to participate in your auction." He walked over to where she held Jenny. When he reached her side, Jenny stretched her arms out to Scott, wanting him to hold her. He took the giggling little girl from Katherine.

"That was very interesting—" His mother stopped in midsentence as she and Cheryl entered the main room, and her gaze landed on Scott holding Jenny and standing next to Katherine. A warm smile curled her lips.

"Well, well, well..." Cheryl's amused voice broke the silence that had suddenly pervaded the room. "...what do we have here? Jenny, who's your new friend?"

A small hand patted Scott on the nose, then on his cheek. "This is Scott. He tickled me and made funny faces." She held up the toy bear. "He gave me Teddy."

Cheryl directed her pleasure toward him. "I wouldn't have believed it if I hadn't seen it with my own eyes. You're some kind of a miracle worker, Scott."

Katherine reached over and tweaked Jenny's nose, causing the little girl to giggle again. "He's definitely the man of the hour." Her gaze settled on his face as she placed her hand on his arm. "I wouldn't have believed it, either."

"Come on, Jenny." Cheryl put her hands out to take

the child from his arms. "It's time for your nap. Say goodbye to Scott."

Tears filled her big brown eyes as she started to sniffle. "I want Scott to tuck me in." She flung her arms around his neck and hid her face.

Scott darted a frantic glance from Cheryl to Katherine, then to his mother. He didn't know anything about children and certainly nothing about little girls. He didn't have the vaguest idea of what to do or how to proceed. In a somewhat less than controlled voice, he pleaded for help. "Will someone do something?"

To his relief, Katherine seized the opportunity. "Of course, Scott can tuck you in, Jenny." She grabbed his free hand and guided him toward the hallway.

The front door swung open with a loud crash, the noise grabbing everyone's attention. Billy charged into the room. "We got trouble!" His voice clearly conveyed the urgency of the situation. "Jenny's ol' lady and that bastard what beat her up are on their way here. You got maybe a minute to hide the kid."

Katherine took immediate charge of the situation. She grabbed Jenny from a startled Scott and handed her to Cheryl. "Take her upstairs and keep her quiet." Her gaze shot to Billy. "Put that knife away and get out of here."

Billy snapped the knife shut and jammed it back into his pocket. "I ain't leavin'. I can take him out"— anger and hostility flashed in his eyes—"without the knife." Billy only stood about five feet nine inches, but Scott had no doubt about his ability to handle himself in any kind of a fight.

"We've got a court order. Jenny's mother can't take her without going into court and proving she's fit

42

to have custody, and that will never happen. Now—"

"All right, give us the kid so we can get out of here." The surly male voice belonged to a man of about twenty, wearing dirty clothes, sporting green hair and numerous tattoos that seemed to repeat a skull and crossbones theme. He swaggered over to Katherine, a small blonde in her late teens following behind him, obviously Jenny's mother. She wore a too-short skirt, low-cut blouse, and no bra.

Katherine held her ground as she glared at the intruder. "I have a court order remanding Jenny to the custody of the center. You can't take her. Now, get out, or I'll call the police."

"Lady, I don't give a damn about your piece of paper. Wanda"—he jerked his thumb toward the blonde woman—"wants her kid back."

"Don't make me laugh." Katherine's tone clearly conveyed the disgust she felt. "The only thing she wants back is the additional welfare money."

Scott quickly sized up Wanda's boyfriend. He stood about the same height as Billy with a slight build. Any man who had to beat up little girls in order to make himself feel big would not take on a bigger man of six feet one inch and almost two hundred pounds. He saw Billy slip his hand inside the pocket containing the switchblade. He quickly stepped between Billy and the intruder, then casually put his arm around the man's shoulders. "There seems to be a little confusion here. Perhaps I can help straighten it out." Offering his friendliest smile, he steered the intruder away from Katherine and his mother, moving him toward the other side of the room.

"We don't need to call the police." Scott's voice

dropped to a near whisper, too low for Katherine and Lynn to hear but not so for Billy who had moved in close to the action. Scott's smile remained in place, and his hand stayed on the man's shoulder as he continued to talk. "We can settle this very simply. I'm an easygoing guy. I'm not into violence. However, that intense young man leaning against the wall"—he indicated Billy who carefully followed every word—"is fully capable of performing open-heart surgery on you and is ready to do just that."

A quick look of uncertainty flashed through the man's eyes as his gaze shot to Billy, then back to Scott towering over him.

"We don't want to get involved in anything that messy, do we? At least, I know I'd rather not." Scott dug his fingers into the young man's shoulder until he flinched from the pain. "And we need to consider the ladies. We wouldn't want to upset them with a lot of blood and violence. We won't even get into a discussion of who would be responsible for cleaning up what would be left of you. I can't speak for anyone else, but I don't care to dirty my hands."

Scott dropped his hand from the man's shoulder and stretched his height to the fullest as he looked down at the unwelcome intruder. "Now, why don't you and your girlfriend take a hike before this whole mess gets totally out of control? There are things you can do to make up for the welfare money that's been cut off. You could get a job." Scott slowly scrutinized the man's appearance. "Of course, I can't imagine for the life of me who would want to hire you." The smile quickly disappeared from Scott's face as his tone turned menacing. "Do we have an understanding?"

The intruder nodded in agreement, his body language telling of his discomfort with the situation. He was alone, backed into a corner by one man who towered over him and another obviously street tough and carrying a knife.

"I didn't hear you. Do we have an understanding?"

"Uh...yeah," the intruder said, conveying a full dose of anxiety.

Scott flashed his smile again as he replaced his hand on the man's shoulder, administering one last painful squeeze. He now spoke at normal volume, loud enough for everyone to once again be able to hear him. "I'm sorry, pal, I didn't catch your name."

"Tom." The word was uttered without enthusiasm.

"Well, Tom. Too bad you and Wanda have to run along before we had a chance to get better acquainted, but it was nice of you to stop by." Scott turned his head toward Billy as he continued to speak. "Aren't you going to say goodbye to our guests? We wouldn't want them to think we were being rude."

"Naw, man. We wouldn't want them thinkin' that." Billy smiled as he sauntered over to Tom. He clamped his hand on Tom's shoulder and gave it the same type of squeeze Scott had used. "Nice seein' ya, Tom."

Tom grabbed Wanda's arm and yanked her along behind him as he hurried out the door, turning to give one last furtive glance in Scott's direction.

Scott turned a very serious look toward Billy. "He's going to be back."

Billy nodded as he gave Scott a new look of respect and admiration. "Yeah, man. You're right."

Chapter Four

"Would someone," Katherine intruded on Scott and Billy's conversation, "be good enough to tell me what just went on here? Why did they suddenly leave without another word about taking Jenny with them?"

"Oh, that." Scott tried to minimize the situation. He gave Billy a quick wink. "We just explained the error of their ways to Tom. He saw the light and decided it was best for all concerned if they left."

She leveled a cool look at Scott. "That's the explanation you're going with? You're not going to tell me what you said to him?"

Scott feigned complete innocence. "Why, *Ms. Fairchild*...I just did. What more do you think there is?"

Her gaze shifted from Scott to Billy who wore the very same expression. "I see I'm not going to get anywhere with you two." She stepped to the hallway and called upstairs. "It's okay, Cheryl. You can come back down now. They're gone."

Cheryl descended the stairs carrying Jenny. She took a quick survey of the room, then turned to his mother who stood quietly taking in everything that had happened. "I hope this little incident doesn't discourage you. I think you'd be a real asset to our organization. I hope you decide to accept my offer."

His mother looked around the room, her gaze resting momentarily on each person present. Everyone

46

seemed to be waiting for her to say something. She glanced around the room one more time. "I taught high school English for almost thirty years. Over that period of time, this type of incident, unfortunately, became an almost daily occurrence." She paused as everyone directed anxious looks at her, everyone except Scott who knew what her answer would be, who knew as soon as he introduced her to the situation that she would want to be involved. "I could start tomorrow if that's acceptable."

Cheryl let out a sigh of relief. "That would be perfect. Welcome aboard."

"Mom, let me introduce you to the rest of the people here. This is Katherine Fairchild. Katherine, this is my mother, Lynn Blake."

The two women shook hands. "It's a pleasure to meet you, Lynn. This is quite a son you have here." Katherine shot him a quick grin. "Full of surprises."

His mother beamed at him. "Yes, he is. Simply full of surprises."

A heated flush rose on his cheeks. He stepped in to quickly change the subject. "Mom, this is Billy Sanchez. Billy, this is my mother, Lynn Blake. She's going to be working here, apparently starting tomorrow." He grinned at Billy, then turned back to Lynn. "You might want to give Billy a description of your car, including the license number. Unless, of course, you don't mind if it disappears off the face of the earth."

"So, you're Scott's ol' lady." Billy circled Lynn, carefully scrutinizing her. "You don't look old enough."

Lynn eyed Billy. Her voice did not hold any anger,

but it did not hold any pleasure, either. "I'm his mother, not his *ol' lady*. Other than that, thank you for the compliment."

Billy slowly nodded, then grinned at her. "You're okay."

What Scott had perceived as a tense moment had been satisfactorily resolved. With a sigh of relief, he addressed his comments to his mother. "I've got to get back to the office. So if you're all set here…"

"Well…" Lynn hesitated.

Katherine quickly jumped into the conversation, directing her comments to Scott. "Why don't you go ahead and take care of your business? We've already taken too much of your time. I can give Lynn a lift to wherever she needs to go."

"Thank you, Katherine." Lynn's expression told Scott she was pleased with the opportunity to stay at the center a little longer.

A tiny voice broke into the conversation. "I want Scott to tuck me in." Jenny wiggled toward him, making it difficult for Cheryl to keep hold of her.

Scott looked at Cheryl with a *what do I do now* expression. Cheryl held the child tighter. "Jenny, Scott has to leave right now. He can tuck you in some other time."

Jenny's eyes brimmed with tears, and her lower lip quivered. "I want Scott to tuck me in." A tear ran down her cheek as she held her arms out toward him.

Reluctantly and very unsure of what to do, Scott took Jenny into his arms and held her. He spoke softly to her. "I've never tucked in a little girl before. Can you tell me what to do?"

All eyes were on Scott as he carried Jenny upstairs.

Katherine didn't know about anyone else's thoughts but hers were definitely of a sensual nature. She allowed her gaze to wander over his handsome features, his broad shoulders, and the way his jeans hugged his hips and long legs. *You may not have any experience tucking in little girls, but I bet you've had lots of experience tucking in big girls.*

Cheryl and Lynn went over Lynn's duties while Katherine busied herself with some paperwork. After fifteen minutes, Scott returned from upstairs. He seemed slightly flustered, the expression on his face a combination of befuddlement and wonder. As he entered the front room, he glanced back toward the stairs, then spoke. "She went right to sleep." He shot his mother a quick glance. "She wanted me to tell her a bedtime story. I don't remember any bedtime stories."

Katherine noted the flush of embarrassment rising on his cheeks. Her first impulse was to tease him about it, but she quelled the urge. "I'm sorry to have imposed on you like that, but it was such a marvelous step forward for Jenny. I didn't want to stop the momentum." Her gaze stayed on his face, then captured his eyes. "Thank you for helping."

"It was no trouble." He glanced around the room. "Now, if you'll excuse me, I need to get back to running a business."

After Scott left, Cheryl and Katherine continued Lynn's orientation on the inner workings of the charity, the other centers and functions, the educational program, and the people involved.

Katherine looked at her watch. Even though it seemed like only a few minutes, a couple of hours has passed. "Oh no, where has the time gone?" She glanced at Lynn. "I'm afraid we've kept you much too long, especially considering that your first workday isn't until tomorrow. I'm so sorry."

"No problem at all. It's been very enlightening."

"Well, I promised you a ride to wherever you needed to go. Are you ready?"

"Actually, Katherine, I live in Marin County. In Tiburon. I'm sure that's completely out of your way. Bay Area Rapid Transit will get me home without any problems. I can take the BART to San Francisco, catch the ferry to Sausalito, then grab the transit bus to Tiburon."

"I won't hear of it. Tiburon is most certainly on my way. In fact—" Katherine thought quickly, trying to come up with a reason to spend more time with Lynn. "—a friend of mine has been raving about a new restaurant in Sausalito, insisting that I give it a try. Tonight would be an ideal time. Could I persuade you to be my guest for dinner?"

Lynn's face lit up at Katherine's invitation. "I'd be delighted."

Katherine made a quick call to the restaurant to make a reservation, then they left the Oakland center and drove to Sausalito.

The two women dined at an elegant little bistro on the waterfront. The evening went by comfortably with both of them enjoying the beginnings of a genuine closeness. They chatted amiably about art, travel, music, current events, even sports, and the often-touchy subject of politics. The time passed much too quickly.

As Katherine pulled the car into the circular drive at Lynn's house, Lynn gathered her jacket and purse, then turned toward Katherine. "Would you like to come in for a cup of coffee?"

Katherine immediately accepted the offer. "I'd love to."

Lynn unlocked the door, and they went inside. "Make yourself comfortable, I'll be right back." She went to the kitchen.

Katherine looked around the room. She felt the love and closeness of the people who had lived there over the years. She picked up framed photographs and studied them. The only photographs in her house as a child were formal family portraits. The photos in Lynn's house were candid pictures taken of people having fun and enjoying their time together. People who obviously loved each other.

She could not remember their family ever taking a vacation together or doing family things just for fun. Her parents went on trips, leaving the children with a governess and housekeeper. Then, during the summer, her parents usually packed her off for a month to a place where the properly brought up little girls of the prominent families went, someplace they called *camp.* But it bore very little resemblance to a place where kids played, got dirty, and, in general, had fun. Only her grandfather had ever tried to give her any semblance of a normal childhood.

Tears sprang to her eyes as memories of those unhappy years flooded her thoughts that, for many years, she had kept locked away in the deepest, darkest recesses of her mind where she would not have to think about them, let alone deal with them. The loneliness, the humiliation…and the numerous beatings. She quickly recovered her composure when she heard Lynn returning from the kitchen.

Katherine stayed for an hour before saying goodnight to Lynn and heading for home.

She pulled her car into her garage. Thoughts and feelings of a warm, happy home and a caring mother circulated through her mind. She envied Scott and what appeared to her to be an idyllic childhood, certainly compared to hers. It had taken a long time for her to overcome her feelings of guilt, humiliation, and anger. As a result, she had always remained distant and reserved with all the members of her family, all except her grandfather. Even now, time spent with her father or her brothers felt stiff, awkward, and very uncomfortable.

Her father had been too busy with his work to notice. Too busy to pay attention to his children. Too busy to pick up on the desperate cries for help from a wife slowly sinking into an emotional abyss. It had been her grandfather who first became suspicious. It had been her grandfather who saved her life—most certainly figuratively and possibly literally.

When her grandfather discovered her mother had been physically abusing her, that she had not been an accident-prone child constantly tripping over this or running into that, her mother had committed suicide rather than face the humiliation and retribution. That had compounded the young Katherine's feelings of guilt and shame.

Her mother had told her she loved her and the punishment was for her own good. Surely, she must have deserved the beatings. Why else would her mother have administered them? Then, when her mother had taken her own life, she knew it must have been her fault. She had been a very bad girl. She must have done something really terrible even though she didn't know what she had done.

She had finally allowed her grandfather to wheedle the truth out of her in spite of her promise to her mother never to tell anyone what had happened. For many years afterward, she had harbored the most sinful guilt of all. She had been relieved when she found out her mother was dead. That meant the beatings would stop. It had been a terrible load of guilt for one little girl to carry. Then in college an ill-fated marriage to a man only interested in the family money...

She had finally come to the realization that to dwell on bad experiences served no purpose. The only thing to do with them was to learn from them. To move on so that she didn't repeat the mistakes and the same experiences did not happen again. The good that had come from her painful childhood was her dedication to the charity. If she could help even one child who had been subjected to similar abuses or, through the charity's educational program, prevent another child from ever having to know those abuses, then something good had come from her awful childhood.

****

Katherine pulled her car up to the curb, noting the three police cars blocking the street. She had gotten the call from Cheryl at five o'clock that morning. She immediately threw on some clothes and drove straight to the Oakland center. She still didn't know exactly what happened. Apparently, Billy had gotten into a fight on the front porch of the center, and someone had been hurt. She didn't know who.

She hurried up the walk to the front door. As soon as she entered the room, she saw Cheryl talking with two policemen and Billy sitting on a chair with another policeman watching him.

When Billy saw her, he jumped to his feet. The words burst from his mouth. "Hey, Kat. It was Wanda and that bastard boyfriend of hers. They came here to—"

"Shut up, Billy," Katherine demanded. "Don't say a word until I get my attorney here."

"But I didn't do nothin'—"

"Shut up!"

Billy took the hint, something that sounded more like a commanding order, and plopped into the chair. His face registered his displeasure at being ordered around. He scowled as she grabbed her cell phone from her purse and made a call without bothering to pause and talk with the policemen.

The call was answered on the fifth ring by an angry man who obviously had been roused from a sound sleep. "This better be important."

"Bob, it's Katherine Fairchild"

"Katherine, do you have any idea what time it is?"

"Yes, I do. I apologize for waking you, but this is important. I'm at the Oakland center. We have trouble here. The police are on the scene. I need you to come over immediately." She pushed as much urgency into her voice as possible. "Hurry."

After a moment's pause, Bob responded, "I'll be there as quickly as I can."

She disconnected from the call and turned to the officer who appeared to be in charge. "Now, what's going on here?"

"I'm Sergeant Caswell, and you are..."

"I'm Katherine Fairchild."

"Are you in charge of this place?"

"For the purposes of whatever is going on here, I'm in charge. This center is run by the Coalition for the Prevention of Child Abuse, and I'm Chairman of the Board of Directors. Now, I repeat my question. What's going on here?" Katherine fixed a very determined stare at the sergeant and waited for him to respond.

"Well, it appears that this young man, who refuses to give us his name, was involved in a knife fight with person or persons unknown. Judging from the blood on the porch and the lack of any wounds on him"—the officer cocked his head toward Billy—"I'd say somewhere out there is a person in need of medical attention."

Katherine looked at Billy, who shot back a look of defiance mixed with just a hint of uncertainty. She returned her attention to the officer. "And where is this other person?"

"We're searching the neighborhood now."

"Are you arresting Billy?"

"We're holding him until we can at least identify him and determine exactly what went on here. You say his name is Billy? We'll be taking him to the station. Any further action will be determined at that time."

"Be very careful how you treat him, Sergeant Caswell. He's only seventeen years old, and that makes him a minor. It will take a judge to determine if he can be treated as an adult." The quick look of caution that crossed the officer's face pleased her, but the moment of triumph didn't last long.

"We're familiar with the juveniles in this neighborhood, Miss Fairchild." He shot another look at Billy. "We're also familiar with their police records."

A few minutes later, Bob Townsend arrived at the center, unshaven, dressed in a pair of jeans and a sweatshirt. "Katherine, what's all this about?"

He pulled her aside, and she gave him a quick rundown of what she knew about what had happened.

"We have a little three-year-old girl, Jenny Hillerman, who has just been placed in our custody by a court order. Yesterday afternoon, the child's mother and boyfriend tried to take her but were thwarted in their attempt. According to Billy, they came back again a few hours later and attempted to grab her, but Billy chased them off after some kind of scuffle. Billy is only seventeen, so he's a minor without any parents. He...he kind of looks out for the people here." She indicated the policeman obviously waiting for them to finish their conversation. "Sergeant Caswell is in charge of the scene."

"Sergeant Caswell, I'm Bob Townsend. I'm an attorney, and I will be representing this young man. You are aware, I believe, that he is a juvenile and should be treated as such. Now, have you already questioned him? If so, did you advise him of his rights?"

"I know who you are, Mr. Townsend." Everyone knew the Fairchild family's highly placed and powerful attorney. "I've questioned him, but he hasn't answered me. I didn't know he was a minor until Miss Fairchild apprised me of the situation a short while ago. He refused to identify himself or give a statement about what happened here."

"If you will excuse me, I wish to confer with my client." Without waiting for a response from the officer, he quickly grabbed Billy and took him into the far corner with Katherine joining them.

"Billy," she spoke with a sense of urgency, "this is Bob Townsend, and he's going to be your attorney. Now, tell us exactly what happened here, and don't leave anything out."

Billy looked at Katherine, glared at Bob Townsend, sat in silence for a long moment, then reluctantly started to talk. "It was Wanda and that Tom guy. I caught him tryin' to break in, and we got into a minor scuffle."

Katherine raised a brow, but before she could say anything, Billy stopped her.

"He ain't hurt that bad. I cut him a couple of times on the arm, and he ran like a scared rabbit." He sneered his contempt. "Anyone who beats up little girls ain't got no stomach for a real fight." He glanced quickly around the room and lowered his voice to a mere whisper as he reached into his shirt pocket and pulled out a piece of paper. "He dropped this."

He handed the paper to Katherine, who scanned the words. Anger boiled inside her as she clenched her jaw, then handed the paper to Bob Townsend.

"Who else was present during that earlier confrontation?"

"Myself, Billy, Wanda and Tom, Lynn Blake, and Scott Blake. I sent Cheryl upstairs with Jenny as soon as Billy warned us, before Wanda and Tom came in the door. Lynn is a new employee here at the center and—"

"Yes, I know who the Blakes are."

Katherine's focus snapped to sharp attention. As soon as the words were out of his mouth, his expression said he knew he shouldn't have said them. Speaking before thinking, an inexcusable thing for an attorney to do. A combination of surprise and anger invaded her reality. She said only one word, but that word spoke volumes.

"Grandpa!" She set her irritation aside for the time being.

"Okay, Katherine. I'm sure I can get him released to the custody of the center with you as the responsible party. With reputable witnesses to the previous incident and the court evidence regarding Jenny, I'm sure there won't be any problems. However, I'm also pretty sure the judge is going to say that Billy either gets a job or goes back to school as a condition for no charges being filed against him."

"Hey," Billy quickly interjected, "I didn't do nothin' wrong. How come I'm bein' treated like someone convicted and bein' put out on parole? Why the conditions?"

"Regardless of why this happened or who was responsible, that switchblade knife you carry is still an illegal concealed weapon." He fixed Billy with a stern look. "You're not out of this yet."

****

Scott pulled up in front of the center. Lynn's car was in the shop, and he had offered to take her to work. Concern and apprehension hit him the moment he saw the police cars. He noted Katherine's car parked at the curb.

"Scott!" Katherine spotted him as soon as he walked in the door. She warmly acknowledged Lynn's presence, filled both of them in on what had happened, then introduced them to Bob Townsend.

"It looks like everyone is through here," Bob said. "They're taking Billy in. I should have him out in a couple of hours, then we'll come back here and discuss this job or school situation." Bob followed the officers out the door.

Even though the note had been given to the officers as evidence, Katherine told Scott about it. "I don't think I'll ever forget the words written on that piece of paper. 'If you want to see the kid again, get $5,000 and leave it in a paper bag on the front porch at midnight tomorrow night.'"

She shook her head as if still trying to comprehend the situation. "And only five thousand dollars…" Her voice became very soft, almost reflective. "I would have paid ten times that…and much more."

"I'm sure they had no idea of the potential. They weren't kidnapping a member of a prominent family. They were snatching her daughter from a charity center. I imagine five thousand dollars seemed like a great deal of money to them."

"Billy obviously interrupted them before they could grab Jenny." She turned an anguished face toward Scott. "I don't understand how someone could do this…."

"Well, *Ms.* Fairchild"—he tried to make his voice teasing, tried to lighten the tension—"I'm sure with your pampered, sheltered upbringing there are lots of things you don't—"

"How dare you presume to know anything about my upbringing." A spontaneous fit of anger lashed out at him as she cut his words off cold. "You don't have any idea what you're talking about." She quickly turned her face away.

Momentary shock left him in stunned silence. What had just happened? He certainly hadn't anticipated that reaction. He grabbed her arm to stop her as she started to walk away. "Katherine?" He didn't know what to say. "I'm sorry if I've upset you. I didn't mean to presume..."

"Forget it." She tried to pull her arm away from his grasp, but he refused to let go.

With his other hand, he lightly brushed his fingertips across her cheek, then lifted her chin until he could look into her eyes. He saw it all—anger, pain, fear, vulnerability—as it crossed her face and reflected in the depth of her eyes. He saw it but didn't understand it.

"I don't think I can forget it." He wanted to reach out to her, take her in his arms, and protect her from everything. This strong, assertive woman suddenly seemed so fragile to him, so in need of someone to take care of her. "Katherine?"

A silent moment of intense emotion passed between them as they stood together. His gaze never wavered as he tried to see inside her soul, tried to read her thoughts. Embarrassment came into her eyes as she finally looked away. He gently lifted her chin again with his fingertips and turned her face back toward him. "What's wrong?"

"Nothing... It's nothing." Kat pulled away from his all too tempting touch. She wanted him to enfold her in his embrace and hold her. She wanted him to make the hurt and anger go away, emotions she was shocked to discover still lived so close to the surface. "I guess I'm just a little tired."

He again turned her face toward him. His gaze delved into her eyes. He took a long moment and seemed to study her. "You may be proficient at a great many things, Katherine Fairchild, but lying isn't one of them."

"Please, I…" She could only force out a soft whisper as she pleaded with him to release her from his spell.

"Let's go get some coffee. Come to think of it, why don't we go and have some breakfast? Bob and Billy won't be back for a couple of hours, and I think you could use a break." He smiled encouragingly. "Come on."

"Well, I guess so…" She glanced around the room and saw Cheryl, Lynn, and two other employees involved with the day's scheduled business. Her expression brightened. "It looks like I'm not really needed here."

"Good. Give me a minute to call my office, then we'll go." Scott pulled his cell phone from his pocket and made a quick call to Amelia, then turned back to Katherine. "Are you ready?"

He placed his hand in the middle of her back as he gently guided her out the door and toward his car. Neither of them said anything as he drove to Jack London Square. Each seemed lost in private thoughts.

Katherine knew she had overreacted to his simple teasing. She had become accustomed to him adding the extra emphasis to Ms. whenever he addressed her, but she had not been prepared for him to attack her background, to bring up her childhood. To humiliate—

What's the matter with you, Katherine? He didn't do any of those things. He had not attacked her background. He had merely tried to lighten the moment. She should apologize, but…

After they were seated at a table in a popular breakfast restaurant, had placed their order, and been given coffee, Scott finally spoke. "What happens with Billy now? What was that business about a job or school?"

She began to relax, her rattled nerves somewhat calmed from the morning's tension. She filled Scott in on everything that had taken place and what Bob suspected would be the outcome for Billy. "I'm not sure how it can all be managed. I've tried several times to get Billy to go back to school, but he flatly refuses. He says he's not going to sit in some classroom with a bunch of kids five years younger than he is." She slowly shook her head. "Frankly, I don't know who would be willing to take a chance on giving him a job."

"The name Fairchild is associated with numerous companies, both as owners and as board members for other corporations. Can't your family find a place for him somewhere?"

A hint of a bittersweet chuckle escaped her throat. "My *family*...my father and brothers don't hold my charitable activities in very high regard. As far as they're concerned, charity is just another word for coddling the lazy. It's like pulling teeth to convince them to make an annual donation to my charity, and I'm sure they only do it because it's tax deductible. In fact, I don't know but suspect my grandfather might be responsible for them giving that contribution. There's no way they would put themselves out to help..."

Katherine became momentarily lost in her own thoughts. The feel of Scott's warm touch as he placed his hand on top of hers brought her back to the reality of the moment. He slowly laced his fingers with hers, the sensation sending tiny shivers of excitement through her body. A shy smile tugged at her lips as she looked into his eyes.

Scott saw Katherine's exposed vulnerability, felt the softness of her hand, experienced the warm sensation that melted inside him. Somewhere deep in his subconscious, he knew he had been caught. She had him hook, line, and sinker. "I think I might know someone who would be willing to take a chance on him."

Her eyes grew wide with anticipation. "Who?"

"Me." Nothing else needed to be said. Her eyes glistened as they misted with happiness. No doubt about it. He was definitely a goner. There remained only the formality of her reeling in her catch as he put up a fight so his capture wouldn't appear too easy. He instinctively knew that any struggle on his part would be useless.

Chapter Five

Scott and Katherine arrived at the center immediately after Bob Townsend returned with Billy. Bob addressed his comments to Katherine while Scott listened. "Billy has been released to the center with you as the responsible party. There's a court date for next week. I've already talked to the assistant district attorney assigned to the case. With the note and the witnesses to the previous incident, we'll be able to get him off with only a short probation. It will definitely be a go back to school or get a job situation."

Bob directed his next comment to Billy, along with a stern look. "Do you understand that? Katherine is responsible for everything you do. You screw up, and the court will come down on her, so you'd better behave yourself and stay out of trouble."

"Yeah, man, I heard." Billy obviously disliked the idea of needing to be answerable to someone...to *anyone*.

Katherine beamed at Scott, then turned toward Bob. "We have a job for him." Billy immediately perked up as she continued. "Scott," her voice radiated her pleasure as she turned a shy but sincere smile in his direction, "has offered to put Billy to work."

Billy jumped up. "Doin' what? Diggin' ditches?"

Scott fixed him with a formidable look, making sure he projected the full force of his authority. "Doing an honest day's work for fair wages. I'm starting a new construction project, a shopping center in San Rafael. I have a trainee program that I run and haven't placed anyone in it yet for this project. You would fit right in it."

"One more thing." Katherine aimed her question at Bob Townsend. "Jenny—am I within my legal rights to take her home with me? As long as Wanda and Tom are on the loose, she's not safe here. The court order says custody of the center. Since I'm chairman of the board, does that extend to my house?"

Bob gave her shoulder a fatherly squeeze. "Sure, I don't think there will be any problem."

Relief spread across her features as she smiled at him.

Scott glanced around the room. Things seemed to be under control. He called across the room to his mother seated at her desk. "Mom, what time do you want me to pick you up?"

Katherine immediately jumped into the conversation. "If you'd like, you can leave your car with Lynn, and I can drop you back in town...or wherever you're going."

Katherine took care of some business while Scott gave instructions to Billy to meet him at his office at seven o'clock the next morning, ready to work. Then Katherine and Scott left in her car and headed across the Oakland Bay Bridge toward San Francisco.

"Do you want me to drop you at your office?"

"I've got a better idea. It's a beautiful, sunny day. Why don't you drop me at the yacht club?" He paused long enough to allow his gaze to slowly move along the entire length of her body and back up to her face. "That is, after we stop at your place so you can change into something appropriate for sailing, then we go to my place so I can do the same."

"Sailing?" Her obvious surprise showed on her face and in her voice. She took her eyes off the road just long enough to glance at him. "You want to take off in the middle of a workday and go sailing?"

"You're a quick study, *Ms.* Fairchild." The teasing tone of his voice spoke volumes. "That's exactly what I want to do. Is it a problem for you?" He reached out and brushed his fingertips against her cheek as he projected his serious concern. "I thought you could use a little diversion. It's been a pretty hectic morning for you."

She held his gaze for a moment, then extended a wide grin as she turned her attention back to the road. "No problem at all, Mr. Blake. No problem at all."

She headed the car toward her house.

Katherine pulled into the garage and preceded Scott through the door into the house. They entered the utility room, then the kitchen. He followed her past the dining room, living room, up a flight of stairs, and into the den on the second floor.

"Make yourself at home. I'll be right back."

She ascended the stairs to the third floor. He slowly and thoroughly took in his surroundings. The huge den had a very comfortable feel. Sliding glass doors led to a large covered balcony with patio furniture and an ocean view. The furniture arrangements in the den divided it into areas of interest. One section was a media center, including a large flat panel television with all the latest toys and gadgets associated with audio and video equipment. Another area contained a pool table. And finally, a wood-burning fireplace tucked away in a cozy corner with a love seat facing it and several large pillows on the floor. The far wall held a wet bar with four barstools.

He stepped into a small hallway and peered through an open door into a tastefully decorated bedroom, obviously a guest room. The door across the hall revealed a full bathroom.

Katherine's voice called down from the third floor, interrupting his inspection tour. "Feel free to look around if you'd like."

"Thanks, that's what I'm already doing." He went downstairs. The formal living room spoke of parties attended by the upper crust of society. The dining room carried the same feel. The large dining table easily seated fourteen people. He saw it as only the best china, silver, and crystal.

The gourmet kitchen felt surprisingly comfortable, enhanced by a sunny breakfast nook in the corner that seated six people. Beyond the kitchen, behind the garage area, were what appeared to be servants' quarters, obviously unoccupied. He found it telling that Katherine Fairchild did not have a live-in housekeeper. He went back upstairs to the den to wait for her. Another five minutes, and she made her appearance.

She stood there looking more delicious than anyone had the right to look. She wore a simple light blue T-shirt and crisp white shorts. Her arms and long shapely legs were nicely tanned. No doubt about it—Katherine Fairchild had the best-looking legs he had ever seen. She wore her hair pulled back at her nape with the top hanging in feathered fringes around her face. Just a touch of color dotted her soft lips. His gaze lingered on those lips.

Katherine broke the awkward silence. She offered him a shy smile. "Well, I'm ready to go."

He gave her directions to his house in Tiburon and tried to keep the conversation light as they drove. "Have you ever been sailing? I'm talking about actual sailing, not boating."

"Yes, I'm well versed in the basics of sailing and can help with some of the simpler operations, but I'm not qualified to take a sailboat out on my own."

"My sailboat should have two people doing the work, but I've been doing this for a long time and am able to handle it by myself. I've also added some new equipment that actually takes over a few of the manual operations."

"Well…" A spontaneous laugh escaped her throat. "Fortunately, I'm a good swimmer."

"You know that swimming is not recommended in San Francisco Bay. Just ask those who attempted to escape Alcatraz." He offered a teasing grin. "If you can find any of them."

****

They pulled into his driveway and quickly entered his house. Scott excused himself and left Katherine in the living room as he went to his bedroom to change clothes.

She wandered around the room. It had the same type of comfortable openness as his mother's house. The room conveyed a strong personality without being overbearing in its masculinity. It also reflected his love of the outdoors and nature. Lynn had told her of his keen interest in ecology and environmental issues the evening they had dinner in Sausalito. She opened the sliding glass door and stepped out onto the deck overlooking the water. The sun warmed her face. Yes, indeed. A beautiful day, perfect for sailing.

Scott watched her for several minutes as she stood at the deck railing. He didn't know how to categorize the many thoughts and feelings coursing through him. He had known more than his share of women, but none like Katherine Fairchild.

In fact, he had almost married Angelina. They even had set a wedding date. In retrospect, he knew the marriage never would have worked. It came as quite a shock to Angelina, however, when he told her the engagement was off. That they were through. He had been temporarily dazzled by her to the point of actually thinking he had been in love. His experience with Angelina had left him with a negative reaction to the social conventions of the rich and famous. Even though his financial status placed him in that group, he did not identify with them. He considered himself as someone who worked for a living rather than living off a trust fund or checking the stock market listings every day.

He continued to study Katherine. She was unique. She…

He allowed his thoughts to fade, or perhaps he shoved them away before they crystallized into some sort of reality.

"I'm all set." Scott's words broke into Katherine's moment of contemplation.

She whirled around, startled back into the here and now. A quick but silent intake of breath passed between her lips when she saw him. He wore casual shorts, a T-shirt, and canvas deck shoes. His broad shoulders, hard chest, and long muscular legs were all very tanned. He apparently spent a great deal of time outdoors, probably on his sailboat. He looked absolutely gorgeous, a fact that did nothing to quell the tremors of excitement becoming increasingly rampant inside her, tremors that made themselves known whenever she was around him.

She stepped in from the deck and closed the sliding door. "This is a very nice room. It has the same feel as your mother's house—warm and comfortable." A sudden embarrassment surged through her. She quickly lowered her eyes, her gaze coming to rest on the floor somewhere between them.

She sensed him standing in front of her, felt the overwhelming power of his closeness. He placed his fingertips under her chin and lifted her face until their eyes met. His sensuality engulfed her to the point where she felt absolutely helpless to resist whatever he might choose to do. The sensation both frightened and excited her. Her breathing quickened ever so slightly.

"You seem to have difficulty with sincere personal moments. They apparently make you uncomfortable." In a voice both soft and caring, he neither teased her nor criticized the shyness and embarrassment she tried to hide. "Why is that?"

Anxiety shivered through her body. She didn't know how to answer his question or, for that matter, if she even wanted to answer it. He was prying into her feelings, fears, and insecurities, things that had taken her a long time to overcome. For many years she had kept them buried deep but finally learned to bring them out in the open and deal with them. She no longer found them frightening. She now understood them. Situations that touched on those dynamics seldom caught her off guard or left her at a loss for words. Scott Blake seemed to have an innate ability to crash right through her exterior and get to the heart of the matter. An unnerving experience prompted by the nearness of this very unsettling man.

"I…" She pulled away from his tantalizing touch and regained her composure. "I really don't know what you're talking about." She offered a dazzling, albeit practiced, smile. "I thought we were going sailing?"

****

An unusually warm autumn day presented itself. San Francisco Bay sparkled in the sunlight as the sleek sailboat moved gracefully through the water and passed under Golden Gate Bridge on its way out to the open sea. Katherine Fairchild remained an enigma to Scott. More than her good looks and sensual throaty voice— her intelligence, poise, delicious sense of humor, and an enticing independence that aroused his senses. All of it in defiance of his preconceived notions.

"Tell me about yourself. I don't know much beyond what I see in the papers and on social media. But just from what I've observed at the Oakland center, I know you're not the person portrayed in the headlines."

He found himself attracted to her directness, her dedication to what she believed in, and her passion for what she deemed to be the right thing to do. He also noted the way she worked hard to hide a shyness at odds with the persona she projected.

"I'm…I'm not sure what you mean." A slight frown wrinkled across her forehead followed by a moment of wariness that clouded her features. "What is it you want to know?"

"Anything you're willing to tell me. How about we

start with why you've dedicated yourself to this particular charity apparently to the exclusion of all the others."

A slight laugh escaped her throat, but it sounded more forced than natural.

"I'm involved in several charities and a regular donator to many different causes." She raised her hand to shade her eyes from the bright sun even though she wore sunglasses. "What a beautiful day, Scott. A perfect day for sailing. You handle this boat with a great deal of expertise. Have you been sailing for a long time? Perhaps on a college sailing team?"

No doubt in his mind, she had just purposely changed the subject. Had he introduced a problematic topic? But why would she be averse to talking about her charitable work? Her efforts on behalf of The Coalition for the Prevention of Child Abuse were widely known. She was becoming more and more of a multilayered mystery. He chose to answer her question rather than pursue his curiosity.

"I've been sailing since I was a little boy. My father owned a sailboat and was an avid sailor. In fact, that's how my mother and father met. He was participating in a regatta, and she was one of the spectators, a beautiful twenty-one who had just graduated from college. He was a dashing *older man* of thirty-two who had already built a successful construction business. It was literally love at first sight."

"I've seen all the photographs in your mother's house, pictures of a happy family doing things together. What a marvelous childhood you must have had, growing up surrounded by so much love."

A haunting moment of sadness covered her, one he didn't understand. They sailed along in silence, the sleek sailboat gliding effortlessly through the water.

She kicked off her deck shoes, stretched her legs out in front of her, and leaned back on her elbows. Her breasts rose and fell with her breathing, the soft fabric of her T-shirt clinging to the delightful fullness of her curves. The breeze ruffled through her hair, causing several strands to wisp across her cheek. The sun pinkened her face as she leaned her head back and closed her eyes. The cries of the gulls mingled with the sound of the wind in the sails.

Even though she seemed at peace, the quick glimpses beneath the façade she so expertly projected continued to linger in his mind. "Penny for your thoughts."

"Oh, I was just thinking how perfect everything is at this moment. I congratulate you on this marvelous idea."

"I'm glad you're enjoying it."

It had been nearly five hours since they left the yacht club. He had wanted to stay out longer, but she reminded him she had to pick up Jenny at the center. She did not want to leave the little girl there overnight. They returned, and he escorted her to her car in the yacht club parking lot.

"I can walk home from here. It's only a couple of blocks. You'd better get going, or you'll wind up in the middle of the late afternoon traffic snarl."

He reached his hand through the opened car window and ran his fingertips across her cheek. "Thanks for going sailing with me. I really enjoyed the day."

"Thanks for asking me. I really enjoyed it, too." Tremors of excitement shot through Katherine as he touched her cheek. Her breathing increased, and her pulse quickened ever so slightly. Their eyes locked in a moment of incendiary desire as he took her face in his hands and leaned toward her. Their lips brushed lightly, then he captured her mouth with his, the intensity of his passion quickly consuming her.

Katherine felt totally lost. She had been anticipating this moment, if she could call a burning desire to feel his lips pressed against hers as merely anticipating something. Perhaps feeling anxious about the inevitable moment would be a better way of describing it. It had only been a matter of time. If he had not taken the initiative, she might have thrown restraint and propriety to the wind and been the aggressor.

His kiss magic, his mouth sensual—she melted under the heat of his passion. Her hand seemed to possess a life of its own. She reached out and caressed his cheek as she returned his intensity. Her heart pounded. The blood surged through her veins. She wanted Scott Blake. She wanted him body and soul.

Scott tried not to succumb to his desires but had been unable to resist her allure. Soft lips that tasted so sweet. He had wanted to kiss her from the moment he stepped into the elevator at the Hyatt and found her there. Every time he saw her only heightened the desire. But in the parking lot of the yacht club? Katherine seated in her car and him leaning through the window? Neither a good time nor a good place, but he had been unable to wait any longer to sample her delicious mouth. The heat of her passion radiated to him from her positive response as she returned his kiss.

He wanted to wrap his arms around her, enfold her in his embrace. But he had to settle for the next best thing. He slipped his tongue between her lips and twined it with hers as he explored the hidden recesses of her mouth. He didn't want this to stop.

She slowly withdrew from the sensual web engulfing them. "I have to go…" The words came out haltingly, and her voice quavered. "Have to get Jenny…need to leave."

"I know," he whispered as he caressed her smooth cheek. She trembled beneath his hand as he caressed her smooth cheek. He looked into her eyes and saw a startling sensuality tempered with just a touch of caution. "Have dinner with me tomorrow night."

Their gazes locked, neither wavering. "I'd love to."

"Good. I'll call you tomorrow afternoon. Will you be at the center?"

"I should be, but if not, try my cell." She handed him a personal business card with her cell number.

He watched as her car moved down the street, around the corner, and out of sight. He walked the short distance from the yacht club to his house, his thoughts filled with the soft sensuality of Katherine Fairchild.

****

Katherine's every thought and breath centered on Scott Blake. It had taken all her conscious effort to pull away from his kiss. He had sent tremors shooting through her body, causing her breathing to quicken and her pulse to race. She had already made one big mistake with men. Did she dare to once again entertain thoughts of a serious relationship, to allow herself an emotional involvement rather than just a physical one? Could she trust her feelings and emotions this time? More than that, could she overcome the bitter taste left from her brief marriage? Would she be able to open her heart to love?

She smiled inwardly as a feeling of calm settled over her. That nineteen-year-old girl from ten years ago had grown up and overcome the major obstacles of her life. She knew the answer to all those questions—an emphatic and resounding *yes*.

Her thoughts snapped into the present. As soon as she picked up Jenny, she would go see her grandfather. She had a few words to share with him about his having Scott investigated. She vacillated between her anger that he would do such a thing to her and her knowledge of why he had done it. In his own way, he was saying he loved her and wanted to protect her. Her anger subsided. She just couldn't stay mad at him, no matter what he did. However, she fully intended to let him know exactly how she felt about it.

She arrived at the Oakland center. As soon as she stepped through the front door, Cheryl called to her. "Kat! Sergeant Caswell is here to see you. I told him I didn't know where you were, but I was sure you'd be here soon."

"Miss Fairchild—" Sergeant Caswell flipped through his small notebook. "—we've gotten a line on Wanda and Tom. Someone answering his description went to an emergency medical care center across town. The doctor fixed him up and told him to come back tomorrow so he could check on the stitches and change the dressing on the wound."

Her spirits lit up at the news. "That's great. Do you think you'll be able to arrest them?"

"When we catch up with them, we will definitely be arresting them. Attempted kidnapping, and if the DA doesn't think he can make that stick, then there's extortion. One way or the other, they won't be on the streets anymore and won't impose a threat to you or the little girl."

"Thank goodness. Then Jenny will be safe. I'm taking her home with me tonight."

"Now, Billy Sanchez—a court date has been set." He flipped the pages in his notebook, unaware of the questioning look Katherine shot at Cheryl or Cheryl's shrug as she shook her head in response, indicating she didn't know where Billy had gone.

"Billy's doing some errands for me right now," Katherine quickly interjected. "He has a job and will be starting work at seven o'clock tomorrow morning."

Sergeant Caswell looked up from his notebook, a momentary hint of surprise in his eyes. "Oh? He already has a job? That was quick. Where will he be working?"

"He has a job with Blake Construction and will be working at the site of a new shopping center being built in San Rafael."

"And this can be verified with Blake Construction?"

"Absolutely. Scott Blake personally gave Billy the job. Billy is to report to Mr. Blake's office at seven o'clock in the morning."

After making the new entries, he closed the notebook. "That seems to take care of my business. Thank you for your time, Miss Fairchild. I'll keep you apprised of the status on Tom and Wanda."

As soon as the officer left the building, Katherine

rushed to Cheryl. "You don't know where Billy is?"

"I haven't a clue. Lynn might know. She was the last one talking to him before he took off." Cheryl glanced at the clock. "She said she had a personal errand to take care of. She should be back in a few minutes."

Katherine packed an overnight bag for Jenny and brought it downstairs. She immediately spotted Lynn coming up the front walk and rushed to talk to her. "Do you know where Billy is? Sergeant Caswell was here asking about him."

Lynn gave her a reassuring smile. "Yes, he's taking care of some personal business. He's just fine. He'll be spending the night here. In fact, he'll be staying at the center until all of this is finished."

"I've been trying to get him to stay here for a long time. How did you manage to talk him into it?"

"I didn't. It was his own idea. He feels he needs to provide protection for the people here."

Katherine expelled a sigh of relief. "As long as that's settled, I'd better get Jenny and go. It's almost her dinner time." She went into the next room to get Jenny, who held tightly to her hand while hugging her new teddy bear. After securing Jenny in the car seat, she drove toward the Oakland Bay Bridge.

Nearly half an hour later, Katherine pulled her car into the circular drive and stopped at the front door of RJ Fairchild's mansion. Carruthers opened the door, and she entered the house with Jenny clutching her hand.

"Grandpa, this is Jenny." The child hid behind Katherine's leg, peeking out to look at the elderly man. Katherine stooped and pulled Jenny into her arms. She spoke very softly to the child. "Can you say hello to Grandpa?" The child took a tentative step toward his wheelchair, bolstered by Katherine's encouragement.

"Hello, Jenny. It's nice to meet you." The old man's voice took on a soft quality. In fact, his entire persona took on a softness not part of his normal demeanor.

Jenny took a second step, then looked back at Katherine, who gave her a warm smile of encouragement. The little girl slowly made her way to the side of his wheelchair, then reached out her hand and patted his arm.

Katherine's eyes glistened with tears of joy as her grandfather picked up the little girl and sat her on his lap. Jenny patted the side of his face and giggled.

The old man seemed genuinely enchanted with her. He pushed the control on the battery-powered wheelchair and started toward the back of the house while talking to her. "Come on, Jenny. Let's take a ride to the garden room and see all the pretty flowers."

With a forthright honesty and openness that only children in the innocence of childhood possess, Jenny asked the powerful patriarch of the Fairchild empire, "Do you know how to make funny faces?"

He chuckled softly as they proceeded down the hallway. "I know how to make grumpy faces, but it's been a long time since I tried to make a funny face."

"Scott makes funny faces."

"Now, who is Scott?"

"He's my friend."

Katherine watched and listened to the exchange. Happiness welled inside her until she thought she would burst. *Who is Scott, indeed. The irascible old coot. He'll soon find out that he doesn't fool me for a second.* She would confront him about the investigation but not now. She followed them down the hallway, happiness totally filling her.

They had dinner, and afterward, Jenny fell asleep on the couch in the den. Katherine took the opportunity to have the private conversation that had been the primary purpose of her visit. "Grandpa, I want to know why you had Scott Blake investigated."

She could tell from the surprised expression that darted across his face before he could hide it that she had caught him completely off guard, which pleased her. It meant she had the upper hand for a change, at least for the moment. But that moment wouldn't last long.

RJ ignored her question, pointing to Jenny sleeping on the couch. "What an adorable child. I can see why you're so attached to her."

"No, you don't, you sly old fox. You're not going to wheedle your way out of this conversation by changing the subject." She gave him a stern look that quickly changed to one of dismay. "How could you do this to me, Grandpa? How do you think Scott would feel if he knew about this?"

His body language told her he realized he had gone too far this time. "Well, Katherine, perhaps I did overstep the boundaries just a bit—"

"Just a bit? How about clearly trespassing, meddling in something that's none of your business, treating me as if I were no older than Jenny? How could you do this to me?" She fought to hold back her tears and the sob trying to work its way out of her throat.

The expression on his face said he knew he

couldn't win this one. It also told her what she already knew that nothing upset him more than seeing her cry, knowing she was unhappy. Especially when he had been the cause of it.

He reached out and took her hand. "I'm sorry, Katherine. I guess I do tend to be a little overprotective. I just don't want to see you hurt again. Forgive me?"

She softened. He had done it again. She could not stay mad at him. "You know I do." She kissed his cheek.

"If it's any consolation, the report gives him a clean slate, first class all the way." He offered up a confident smile, one that said he hoped the information pleased her.

"Speaking of the report, I want all the copies you have. I know it will be safer in my hands. Now—hand them over." She waited patiently while he reluctantly went to his desk and removed a folder with *Scott Blake* printed on the tab in large block letters.

She shoved the file folder into her large shoulder bag, said goodbye to her grandfather, picked up the sleeping child, and drove home.

She started to put Jenny into the guest room, then hesitated. What if she woke up during the night, was all alone, and didn't know where she was? She would probably be frightened. Katherine took her upstairs and tucked the little girl securely into her bed, then took Jenny's teddy bear from her shoulder bag. She smiled warmly as she thought of Scott buying it as a present for Jenny. She carefully placed it under the little girl's arm.

Katherine bent and gave the sleeping child a loving kiss on the cheek, then smoothed her hair back from her face. "Good night, Jenny. May the rest of your life be filled with only pleasant dreams." She turned out the light and left the room.

She hesitated a moment after pulling the file folder out of her shoulder bag. She started to open it. Her grandfather had said Scott had a clean slate, first class all the way. Her curiosity overcame her reticence, and she flipped open the report and started reading.

Halfway through the first page, she abruptly closed the folder and tossed it onto her desk. No, she would not pry into his background. It had taken a lot of time, not to mention the thousands of dollars spent with an analyst, for her to retrieve her self-esteem from the place she had buried it, a place so deep inside her that it had been almost too painful for her to dig it out. But dig it out she had. She had learned to trust her emotions and instincts, to stand up for herself, to be strong. She would not allow the old feelings of insecurity and uncertainty to get a new foothold and take root again.

The chilly night sent a shiver across her skin as she stepped out onto the third-floor deck off her bedroom. She still wore her shorts and T-shirt, even though the sun had been down for several hours. She sipped from her glass of wine while reflecting on the events of the day. What had started out as an absolute disaster before it was even daylight had turned into the most marvelous of afternoons. Scott represented everything she had ever wanted, everything she needed in her life. She closed her eyes and allowed images of Scott Blake to dance across the screen of her mind.

Chapter Six

After Katherine left him at the yacht club, Scott had walked home and waited for his mother to return his car, then he took her to the mechanic's garage to pick up her car. They discussed the events of the morning while driving.

"Billy is really looking forward to working for you. He'll never say so, but I could see it in his eyes every time he mentioned it. And he mentioned it several times. What are you going to have him do?"

"I thought I'd just turn him over to John Barclay. I called John while waiting for you and filled him in on the situation, and he's okay with it. He's the foreman on the project and in the best position to know where Billy would work out. Besides, he has a son about Billy's age, which might give him some insight into Billy. I've asked him to keep the circumstances of Billy's employment confidential. There's no reason for the entire crew to know."

"I'm really proud of you, Scott. This is a very nice thing you're doing."

"Come on, Mom. It's no big deal. The kid's had a rough go of it and deserves a break. Besides, I'm not *giving* him anything. I expect him to work for his money just like any other member of the crew."

"That's not exactly true. You're giving him an opportunity, a chance to prove himself and get out of the place where he's been stuck for seventeen years, and I think Billy is smart enough to realize it even if he doesn't say so." She reached over and brushed an errant lock of hair from his forehead. "It looks like you picked up some sun today. Did you go sailing?"

"Yeah, I went out for a few hours. Much too nice a day to pass up."

She smiled knowingly. "I thought so. That would certainly explain Katherine's shorts and T-shirt when she picked up Jenny, along with the evidence of her having spent the day in the sun."

He groaned and shot his mother a quick glance, then a wry grin. "I can't have any privacy, can I?"

"I wasn't prying, dear…just observing."

After dropping Lynn off at the mechanic's, Scott returned home, grabbed a bite to eat, then settled into the corner of the living room couch with a book. After ten minutes, he closed the book and set it aside. Shaking his head in exasperation, he abandoned any attempt at reading. He had read the same page several times yet didn't have the vaguest idea what was written there. He found it impossible to concentrate on the book.

He saw Katherine's face superimposed on the page—her sparkling turquoise eyes, finely sculpted features, and absolutely delicious mouth. He could not speak for her, but that kiss had scorched him all the way down to his toes. How was it possible for that delightful package of brains, beauty, and sensuality to still be single?

After making another futile attempt at reading, he finally gave up and went to bed.

Scott arrived at his office very early the next

morning to sort through the paperwork that had accumulated on his desk during his absence yesterday. Amelia had rescheduled his only appointment. By the time he finished organizing his desk, he heard someone in the outer office.

"Billy? Is that you?"

"Yeah." Billy sauntered into Scott's office. "So this is where you work." He eyed the surroundings, taking in everything, then turned his attention to Scott. "This is all you do? Sit here pushin' paper around a big desk?"

Scott suppressed a grin. No question about Billy being way out of his element and trying his best to be nonchalant, to not show he was impressed with what he saw. "Sometimes I'm in meetings or out at one of the construction sites. You're going to be working at a site in San Rafael where we're starting construction today on a new shopping center." A sudden thought struck him. He shot Billy a serious look. "How did you get here this morning?"

Anger flashed in Billy's eyes before he snapped, "What difference does it make? I'm here, and I'm on time."

"You hitchhiked, didn't you?" Scott fixed him with a hard stare, refusing to break eye contact.

Finally Billy turned away, his voice much quieter. "Yeah, I hitched. So what's the big deal?"

"I can't have you trying to bum a ride from Oakland to San Rafael every day. There's no way of guaranteeing that you'd be on time for work." Scott reached into his pocket, took out three twenty-dollar bills, and handed them to Billy. "Here, take the BART from Oakland to San Francisco, then catch Golden Gate transit to San Rafael. You'll also need to buy your lunch. You can't spend all day at a construction site doing physical labor without eating something."

Billy glared defiantly at him. "I ain't takin' no charity. I told you I'd be to work on time, and I will."

"Charity?" He suppressed the amused grin that tried to take hold. "Not a chance. I expect you to pay back every penny of this sixty dollars out of your first paycheck." Scott shoved the money into Billy's shirt pocket. "Now, let's go, or you'll be late for your first day's work."

For a long moment, Billy stood staring at the floor. He finally looked up at Scott, then turned and headed out the door, the money still in his pocket. Billy didn't need to say a word, Scott saw it all in his eyes. No one had ever given him a break. He didn't know how to respond to the situation or how to show his appreciation.

On the way to the construction site, Scott filled Billy in on how things would work. He would report directly to John Barclay with John being the only one who knew the circumstances of his employment. The rest of the crew would be told that he was part of the Blake Construction trainee program. After getting Billy situated, Scott went back to his office to take care of the day's workload.

****

Katherine's morning started by getting Jenny up and into the bathtub. Jenny giggled as Katherine blew the bubbles off her little hands. After her bath, Katherine helped Jenny out of the tub and dried her off. She started to help her dress, but Jenny informed her that she was a big girl and could dress herself. Katherine kissed her on the cheek and waited patiently as the child struggled with the clothes.

Then she busied herself in the kitchen fixing breakfast for the two of them. She had been correct in her decision to move the little girl from the guest room to her bedroom. Twice during the night, Jenny had awakened from a bad dream. Katherine had been right there to comfort her and see that she got back to sleep.

Jenny tried her best to be a big girl, to show her independence. Despite the horrible circumstances of the first three years of her life, she displayed an incredible inner strength and determination. Tears welled in Katherine's eyes as she wondered what the future held for Jenny.

****

The day seemed to pass quickly for all concerned. At precisely seven o'clock that evening, Scott pulled into Katherine's driveway. He had made dinner reservations at an upscale restaurant with a city view. He wore a new suit in honor of the occasion. The prospect of spending the entire evening with her excited his senses, and afterward...well, perhaps nature would take its own course.

"Cheryl!" Genuine surprise caught him when he saw her standing on the other side of Katherine's front door.

She greeted him warmly and stepped aside so he could enter the house. "I'm staying with Jenny while you and Kat have dinner. Tom and Wanda are still on the loose. Kat doesn't want to leave Jenny at the center overnight until they're in custody."

"Scott?" Katherine's voice floated down from somewhere upstairs. "I'll be there in just a minute. I want to get Jenny settled in bed."

A little voice called out, the excitement unmistakable. "Scott, Scott...I want Scott to tuck me in."

He glanced at Cheryl who chuckled and shrugged. "I guess you've been summoned." She pointed up the stairs. "Third floor."

Jenny ran across the bedroom toward the door when she heard him coming up the stairs. "Scott...Scott."

He knelt as the giggling child ran to him and threw her arms around his neck. He picked her up and rose to his feet as he glanced casually around the room. Katherine's bedroom—tastefully decorated, a feminine quality without being frilly. The entire third floor seemed separate from the rest of the house. He noted the deck, a door that opened into a bathroom, and another door that opened into what appeared to be an office.

Then his gaze fell on Katherine. She wore a turquoise silk dress that brought out the color of her eyes, the hem falling just above her knees, her shoes the same color. Her lustrous black hair piled high on her head in the same manner as the first time he had met her when she came to his office to confront him about participating in the bachelor auction. An elegant diamond necklace adorned her neck, no doubt in his mind that it was real. She wore matching earrings to complete the look. His breathing increased ever so slightly as excitement sizzled across the open expanse.

He carried Jenny across the room and gently deposited her on the large bed. "I want to go with you." Big brown eyes looked up at him, questioning eyes wide with innocence.

He pulled the covers up around her. "You can't go tonight, Jenny. But"—he looked questioningly at Katherine—"tomorrow is Saturday. Maybe we can all go on a picnic. Would you like that?" He wasn't sure exactly where he had directed his remarks, to Katherine or Jenny.

"Doesn't that sound like fun?" Katherine sat on the edge of the bed next to Jenny. She casually brushed the little girl's blonde curls away from her face. "Would you like to do that, Jenny?"

"A picnic! A picnic!" Jenny excitedly clapped her hands as her face beamed her pleasure.

"Then that's what we'll do." Katherine bent over and kissed the giggling child on the cheek. "You be a good girl for Cheryl tonight."

Scott drove them to the restaurant where they were seated immediately. He ordered champagne, then they placed their dinner orders.

"I got Billy settled into his job this morning."

"Was he on time? I worried about how he was going to get there, especially by seven o'clock in the morning. I even offered to come pick him up, but he refused."

"He was on time. He hitchhiked. I told him I couldn't have him depending on catching a ride all the way to San Rafael every morning." He chuckled as he recalled Billy's uncomfortable moment about the sixty dollars. "I gave him some money and told him to take the BART. I made it clear that it was a loan, not charity, and I expected him to pay me back. For a moment, I thought he was going to refuse, but he finally left with the money in his pocket."

"Do you think this job will work out for him? That

he'll actually apply himself?"

"I checked with John Barclay this afternoon, and he said Billy seemed to be paying attention and doing what was expected of him."

"How did you get into the construction business? I know your father founded the company, but your mother told me your college education was certainly along other lines."

"My grandfather owned a very large area of land, several thousand acres that was primarily pasture land. He had started a small construction company. The state wanted to build a highway across the land. My grandfather agreed to the sale of that portion of the property predicated on his company building the highway. And the rest, as they say, is history and leads us to the company as it stands today."

"And your mother? Did Lynn work as a school teacher all those years?"

"Teaching school is what she always wanted to do. Before she accepted his proposal, she made my father agree to let her teach, even though they didn't need that additional income, rather than her being a stay-at-home wife."

He tilted his head and gave her a questioning look. "What about you? What did you study in college? Did you have any career plans of your own, or had you intended to work in one of the family businesses?"

The hint of discomfort flashed across her face followed by the same type of wariness he had seen when they were sailing and he had casually inquired about her background. The waiter arrived with their dinner, putting an end to his attempt to learn more about her.

****

"This is lovely, Scott." Katherine placed her fork on her plate after taking the last bite of her dinner.

He could not take his eyes off her. The flickering candlelight created soft, dancing shadows that played over the creamy texture of her skin. They held each other's gaze for a long moment, lost to the powerful depth of feeling that had been building between them all evening.

The busboy broke the spell when he cleared the dishes, and the waiter inquired about dessert. Katherine and Scott declined, claiming to be too full. Then she glanced at her watch. "I really hate to put an end to this evening, but it's getting late. I need to let Cheryl go home. Her husband is probably fit to be tied by now."

They relinquished the table and left the restaurant. Scott pulled into her driveway, turned off the engine, reached his arm around her, and pulled her to his side. "Thank you for having dinner with me."

He ran his fingertips across her cheek and down the side of her neck. She tilted her face up toward his. Her eyes sparkled, her lips slightly parted. He lowered his head, captured her mouth, and tasted the same sweetness he had previously enjoyed.

Katherine's pulse raced as her breathing quickened. The spell of his magnetic sensuality settled over her. No one had ever made her feel the way he did, touched her very soul the way he did at that moment. She reached her arms around his neck, running her fingers through his thick hair where it lay across his nape.

She returned all the passion of his kiss as her tongue twined with his. Wild surges of desire swept through her body. Her heart pounded, and her breathing became labored. His mouth—soft and sensual yet at the same time insistent. She gladly gave everything it demanded. To her dismay, he broke off the kiss. He cupped her face in his hands, his gaze intent as he looked into her eyes. Sensual waves swept through her body.

"I feel like a teenager making out in the car. Any minute now your father is going to flip the porch light on and off as a signal for you to get inside the house." His thick voice matched the sound of his ragged breathing. He touched slightly trembling fingertips to her lips, let out a soft groan, then released her from his embrace.

He opened the car door for her and held out his hand to assist her. He continued to hold her hand as they walked to the front door of her house. After unlocking the door, she turned to him. "Would you like to come in for an after-dinner drink?"

Butterflies fluttered around in her stomach. She felt more like a teenager on a first date with the most popular boy in school than a sophisticated woman of twenty-nine.

"I'd like that very much."

Katherine called out as they entered the house, "Cheryl, we're back." They went upstairs to the den.

Cheryl came down from the third floor. "I was just checking on Jenny. She woke up earlier, another bad dream."

Katherine frowned slightly as she slowly shook her head. "I was hoping the bad dreams would have stopped by now. The poor little thing, she still doesn't feel safe and loved."

She knew how long it had been when she was a

little girl before she had been able to sleep through the night without the nightmares returning, how much time had passed before she had completely buried the pain, only to have to resurrect it again during therapy. A resurrection, however, that had been worth every painful minute. She spoke in a whisper, more to herself than to anyone else. "I wonder if she'll ever feel safe and loved."

Scott's arm slipped around her shoulders, followed by a quick squeeze. The comforting gesture provided her with a warm feeling of belonging, a moment that told her just how important Scott Blake had become to her life in such an incredibly short amount of time.

Cheryl pulled on her jacket and grabbed her purse from the table. "Well, I'd better get home before Dan locks me out."

Scott immediately started for the stairs. "It's late. Let me walk you to your car."

Cheryl smiled graciously. "That's most gallant, sir, but it won't be necessary. It's at the curb right in front of the house. Good night." She headed down the stairs and out the front door.

Scott took off his suit jacket, draped it across the back of the love seat, and loosened his tie before sitting down. Katherine tried to suppress her grin. "Feel free to make yourself comfortable."

"I think I'd feel more comfortable if you joined me." He patted the seat cushion next to him as his look captured hers. "Why don't you come over here and sit down?"

Tremors rippled through her as she moved toward the love seat. "Oh? Are you getting ideas?" Her heart pounded, and her breathing quickened.

"Nope, not *getting* ideas. I've already got them."

There was nothing subtle about the sexual tension that permeated the room like a whirling vortex capturing everything in its path. She felt light-headed as he reached out and grasped her hand, drawing her down next to him.

Neither of them spoke. Words seemed so unnecessary, almost an intrusion into the sensual veil enveloping them. His mouth seized, nibbled, devoured. She became lost in his sensual aura. Nothing else mattered at that moment.

"Mommy...mommy..." Jenny's screams ripped through the house, instantly throwing cold water on the heated passion that had rapidly built between them.

"Jenny!" She pushed away from Scott and ran from the room. Her heart pounded but not from her inflamed desires. Another nightmare had invaded Jenny's sleep. She knew very well what the nightmares were. She used to experience the same type of nightmares that woke her up screaming in the middle of the night. She knew how frightening they were for the little girl.

She sat on the edge of the bed, wrapped her arms around Jenny, and gently rocked her. "It's okay, Jenny. I'm here with you. You're not alone." She continued to hold the sobbing child.

****

It had all happened so fast. One moment Scott had a soft, sensual, and very desirable woman in his embrace, driving him into a frenzy. The next moment, he found himself alone. He went to Katherine's bedroom door and watched as she rocked Jenny in her arms. She continued to talk to the child in whispers, apparently oblivious to his presence.

"It's okay, Jenny. No one is going to hurt you. You're safe." A look of pain and anguish crossed Katherine's face, then changed into a hardened determination. "I know what's happening inside you, what you're going through. I know about the nightmares. I promise you no one will ever hurt you again. I won't let them."

Her words jolted him. He didn't know what to make of them, how to interpret their meaning. Too many loose pieces surrounded Katherine's life, pieces he didn't know how to put together. He watched as she continued to hold Jenny in her arms and rock her even though the little girl had stopped crying and appeared to be sleeping again.

"Is she okay?"

Katherine looked in his direction, obviously startled by the sound of his voice. "I…I didn't hear you come up the stairs. Yes, she's sleeping."

She tucked the covers around Jenny. The little girl looked so peaceful and angelic. No one would ever suspect she had just experienced another nightmare. He took Katherine's hand and led her from the room.

"How about you? Are you okay?"

"Me? Why, of course I'm okay." A hint of anxiety crossed her face as she nervously glanced around, but it quickly disappeared. The moment left him a little unsettled, but he didn't know why.

He placed his fingertips under her chin and lifted her face until he could look into her eyes. She did an excellent job of hiding whatever was troubling her. Then his mouth claimed hers. Not with the demanding passion of earlier but rather with a soft kiss of gentle caring.

"You're a very special lady, Katherine Fairchild."
He looked into the depths of her eyes for a long
moment, searching for some sort of answer to his
unasked question. Finally, he spoke again. "Why don't
you and Jenny meet me at my house about ten-thirty
tomorrow morning? We'll take the ferry to Angel
Island from Tiburon and have our picnic."

She smiled. "We'll be there."

Scott retrieved his coat. The mood and the sensual
spell had been broken. He reluctantly left her house.

****

Saturday morning found Billy at Lynn Blake's
house. He slammed the book closed. "Jeez, I can't do
this. It's no use."

Lynn gave him a stern look. "Yes, you can. All you
have to do is apply yourself. You're obviously smart.
You'd have to be to have survived on the streets since
you were thirteen without getting into drugs or ending
up in a juvenile detention center. Now, young man"—
she tapped the cover of the book—"get to it."

"Mom?" Scott's voice came from the front room.
"Are you home?" His voice drew closer as he walked
through the house toward the kitchen.

Billy quickly shoved the books and papers across
the kitchen table and jumped to his feet. "Jeez, what
next?"

Lynn answered Scott. "In the kitchen."

"I need to borrow…" Scott's gaze landed on Billy.

"Borrow what, dear?"

Scott wrinkled a brow in confusion. "I'm not
interrupting anything, am I?"

"Not at all. Billy volunteered to help me with a few
things. We were just discussing what needed to be

done."

Scott noted the quick look of relief that crossed Billy's face. His mother offered no further explanation, and Billy said nothing. He decided to let the matter drop, for the time being. "I want to borrow the picnic basket…" He glanced down at the floor. "And a picnic lunch to go with the basket."

When he looked back at his mother, her eyes sparkled with unconcealed amusement. "A picnic lunch? For how many people?"

"Two…no, three…actually two adults and one child."

Not only did his obvious embarrassment amuse his mother, but Billy seemed to be clearly enjoying Scott's discomfort.

An hour later, Scott returned home and prepared for his outing with Katherine and Jenny.

He carried the picnic basket, and Katherine held Jenny's hand as they boarded the ferry that went from Tiburon to Angel Island, a state park located in San Francisco Bay. He had been surprised by Katherine's appearance—a pair of old, faded jeans, a T-shirt, and sneakers. She had fixed her hair in a French braid and, again, wore only a hint of makeup.

She seemed very far removed from the proper socialite who had confronted him in his office. He marveled at how she had touched his life, how their lives had become so interconnected, how she caused things to happen, starting when she had actually been able to persuade him to participate in the bachelor auction.

He had been trying for a long time to get his mother out of the house and involved in something, and now she had accepted a job at the center, something she said she found very fulfilling. Billy had entered his trainee program at the construction site and apparently had agreed to help his mother with something. Life was, indeed, strange.

When they got to the picnic site, Scott spread the blanket on the ground under a large tree. They had decided against the picnic table, preferring what Katherine had called *an old-fashioned picnic*. After lunch, they took a walk along one of the wooded trails. The sun filtered down through the trees, creating mottled patterns of light and shade on the ground. The gentle breeze rustled the leaves.

He held Katherine's hand as they strolled along the path. Jenny would run ahead of them, hide behind a tree, then jump out as they approached. She'd say, "Boo!" then giggle and run ahead again.

"Oh, Scott, for the first time in her life, she can run, play, and laugh the way all children should." A look of sadness covered her face. "I wonder what's going to happen to her, if she'll ever have a real home and a family to love her."

He immediately recognized the look as the same one he had seen on her face at other times. He squeezed her hand, then brought it to his lips. "I'm sure she'll be fine. She has you, doesn't she?"

Katherine gave him a shy smile, then leaned her head against his shoulder as they continued to walk.

Twenty minutes later, Jenny snuggled in the picnic blanket as Katherine handed her the teddy bear. Not only was it past time for her nap, she had completely worn herself out on their romp in the woods. Scott had carried her back to their picnic site. In a matter of moments, she fell sound asleep.

Scott sat down with his back against the tree and his long legs stretched out in front of him. Katherine sat between his legs, her back against his chest, his arms around her waist, and his cheek against her head. She rested her hands along the outer edges of his thighs. Neither spoke for a long time as they enjoyed their closeness.

****

Katherine felt so comfortable with him, being in his arms felt so right. She allowed her mind to wander back to the previous night, to where things might have gone if Jenny had not had the nightmare that put an end to their heated moment of passion. She had engaged in discreet sexual relationships since her divorce, always mindful of not doing anything that would give the tabloids and various social media outlets a salacious story. None of her physical relationships had included an emotional investment. But this was different, very different. Being with Scott would be something very special. Being with him forever was what she wanted most.

"I'm so worried, Scott."

"Worried about what?" He placed a tender kiss on her cheek, then a teasing chuckle escaped his throat. "If you're concerned about it raining on our picnic, I think we're safe. Blue sky, bright sunlight, and nary a cloud in sight."

She allowed a shy smile. "No, that's not my concern." She twisted in his arms until they were face-to-face. "I'm worried about Jenny, about her future. She can't stay at the center until she's eighteen. And even if she could, what kind of a life is that for her? The courts usually try to return children to their home if at all possible, but I won't allow that to happen to her. She needs somewhere safe to live."

"She has you. How could she have a better home than that?"

"She needs more than that. She needs a *real* home with a mother and a father who love her, a yard where she can play."

Anguish and anxiety shivered inside her, the result of the inner turmoil she had not been able to hide. He pulled her closer as the tremor ran through her body. Then his mouth captured hers—a kiss of tender emotion escalating toward heated passion.

The sound of a tiny voice intruded into the moment. "You guys are kissing," followed by a series of giggles. It had been a little over two hours since Jenny had fallen asleep. The moment she woke from her nap had gone unnoticed by Katherine and Scott who were involved in the delicious sensations of a romantic kiss. As romantic as possible in a public place in the middle of the day.

It had been a long day for the little girl, one filled with exciting new things. They returned to Tiburon, and Katherine retrieved her car from Scott's house.

Jenny yawned, obviously trying to stay awake so she wouldn't miss anything. Katherine drove them back to her house, carried the little girl upstairs, and tucked her into bed. She turned out the lamp, pulled the blanket up around Jenny's shoulders, smoothed the blonde curls away from the little girl's face, then slipped the teddy bear under her arm. Seating herself on the edge of the bed, she watched Jenny sleep.

The afternoon had solidified Katherine's feelings

about Scott. He had become her one burning desire in life. She found herself suddenly surrounded by all the things she never had, all the things she thought she would never be able to have, the things that money can't buy. An intelligent, warm man whose mere presence filled her with excitement. His caring mother to replace the mother she never had. A child, a darling little girl, who truly needed her.

Never in Katherine's entire life had anyone ever really *needed* her just for herself. No one except her grandfather had even cared about her. Hopefully, Jenny would be able to sleep through the night without the bad dreams returning. Then Katherine kissed her tenderly on the cheek and left the room.

****

The phone woke Katherine from a sound sleep. She squinted at the clock—five-thirty on Sunday morning. She glanced over at Jenny. The little girl was still asleep. She tried to clear the grogginess from her head, to dismiss the highly erotic dream about Scott that continued to swirl through her mind.

She grabbed the phone from the nightstand next to the bed. "Hello."

"Miss Fairchild?"

She didn't recognize the man's voice. She sat upright, wide awake with her senses on alert. "Who's calling?"

"This is Sergeant Caswell, Miss Fairchild."

A tremor of anxiety jolted her. "Yes, Sergeant Caswell, what can I do for you?"

"We need someone to make a positive identification."

"Identification?" Her voice quavered, and her body

trembled.

"It's Tom and Wanda. They went back to the emergency care center to have the dressing on his wound changed. One of our patrol cars spotted them. They were on a motorcycle and tried to get away. Apparently, Tom lost control of the motorcycle. There was an accident..."

Her stomach churned and tied in knots as she listened to Sergeant Caswell. "Certainly. I'll be there as soon as I can make arrangements for someone to look after Jenny." She disconnected the call. For a moment, she stood motionless next to her bed, not quite sure what to do. She could not leave Jenny alone, and she certainly could not take the little girl with her to the morgue.

She picked up the phone and dialed Scott, quickly explained the situation, and asked if he could stay with Jenny.

Katherine dressed, being very quiet so she wouldn't wake Jenny. She nervously paced up and down the kitchen, drinking coffee and waiting for Scott. He had agreed to come right over. After what seemed an eternity, she heard a car pull into her driveway. She rushed to the door.

"Lynn!" She stepped aside to let Scott and his mother come in, noting both of their cars in her driveway.

"I brought Mom along." Scott took immediate control of the situation. "She's going to take Jenny back to her house and keep her there."

Lynn gave Katherine a comforting smile and a little hug. "Don't worry about anything. She can stay at my house tonight, and I'll bring her to the center tomorrow morning when I go to work. Now, show me where her things are."

Confusion hit Katherine, leaving her perplexed. "Well…"

"Show Mom where Jenny's things are." Scott had not asked a question. He had informed her of his decision. "I'm going with you. I don't want you doing this alone."

Chapter Seven

Scott parked in Katherine's driveway. She had not uttered a word the entire ride back from the morgue. They entered the house and went upstairs to the den. She collapsed onto the love seat and just sat there. She felt as if she couldn't wake up from a bad dream, couldn't stop the images from swirling around in her mind. Scott sat next to her, put his arms around her shoulders, and pulled her against his body. She gratefully took the strength and comfort he provided.

She finally managed to say something, as much to herself as to him. "The entire time she's been at the center she's never once asked where her mother is or when she would be back. Only in her nightmares does she ever call out to her." She turned toward Scott, anguish coursing through her body. "What can I say to her? How can I tell her that she will never see her mother again? That her mother is never coming back?"

Her unanswered questions hung heavily in the air. Her body trembled from the emotional turmoil as he held her close. "I don't know. Even if you found the words, would she understand? Perhaps it would be best if you waited. Give it a little time…for both of you."

She reached up and grasped the hand resting on her shoulder. She tried to bring back the words used to tell her that her mother was never coming back. Of course, she had been ten years old, much older than Jenny. To a three-year-old, death was an abstract concept, an understanding not easily grasped. Perhaps Scott was right, maybe it would be better to wait for a while, especially since Jenny had never asked for her mother. She gave his hand a squeeze as she looked into his face, offering him a shy smile. "I'm sorry to have called you at such an awful hour, but I really appreciate you insisting on going with me. I know I would have been able to do that by myself, but I'm so relieved that I didn't have to."

"I'm glad you called me." He kissed her on the cheek and held her in his embrace for a moment longer. "It's almost lunchtime. I don't know about you, but I haven't had any breakfast. I didn't even get any coffee. How about we go out and get something to eat?"

"Why don't I fix us something to eat right here? I don't really feel like going out." She slipped from his embrace and rose to her feet.

"Brains, beauty, and can cook, too? Why, *Ms.* Fairchild, how is it that some lucky man hasn't snapped you up before now?" His teasing grin faded when she couldn't hide her feelings fast enough. "What's wrong?"

She reached her hand out toward him. Someone had *snapped her up*. Someone who had turned out to be a cold, unfeeling gigolo who had used her. A man who had not really cared about her at all. She hastily withdrew her hand, dismissing the memory and regaining her composure. Her practiced smile quickly covered her face. "Nothing's wrong. I just think you should reserve your opinion about my cooking until after you've tasted it." She laughed. "You could be in for a rude awakening."

He looked at her, the intensity in his eyes making her feel as if he could reach inside her and drag out all her secrets.

"That doesn't answer my question." He smoothed her hair away from her face. A ripple of desire raced across her skin. "How is it possible for you to still be single? Have you ever been married?"

He had rejected her attempt to change the subject and asked her a direct question. *Tell him it's none of his business? Lie to him?* Or do what she knew she had to do—tell him the truth. For them to have any kind of a future together, she had to be honest with him. At least as far as what he had specifically asked. But the rest of it… She wasn't ready to deal with it yet.

She sucked in a steadying breath in an attempt to calm her rattled nerves. "Yes. I got married when I was a sophomore in college. It only lasted a few months."

"What happened?" The sincerity covering his face, the tenderness in his voice… He wasn't digging for juicy details or trying to pry into her life. It was a genuine attempt to bring them closer together.

"It was an impulsive and stupid action. It didn't work out. We got quietly divorced, and I never saw him again." The rest of the story would have to wait until she felt more comfortable talking about it.

"What about you? Have you ever been married?"

"Married? No, but I was engaged for a while."

"What happened?"

He allowed a soft chuckle. "As you said, it didn't work out."

She flashed a dazzling smile. "I'm glad, otherwise you wouldn't have been eligible to participate in our bachelor auction, and I probably never would have met you." With that, she hurried downstairs to the kitchen, hoping he'd let the subject go.

After eating, they took their coffee up to the den. She put on some soft music while he headed for the fireplace. The beautiful weather of just a few days ago had given way to a storm front. "It feels like it's going to rain. There's nothing like a cozy fire on a dreary day." In a matter of minutes, he had the flames dancing over the logs.

Katherine seductively slipped her arms around his neck and brushed her lips against his. "You're a very nice man."

His eyes widened in mock surprise. "Why, *Ms.* Fairchild—if I didn't know better, I'd swear you were trying to seduce me." His breathing quickened ever so slightly as she ran her hand across his nape and tickled her fingers through his thick hair.

She brushed her lips against his again, then softly teased, "Why, Mr. Blake, whatever would make you say a thing like that?"

Their gazes locked for an instant, then she removed her arms from around his neck and took a step back. He grabbed her arm, pulled her against his body, and held her tightly. "Don't start something you're not prepared to finish." His husky voice conveyed the depth of his passion.

She trembled in his arms as she rested her head against his chest. "I was prepared to finish it Friday night." Her voice came out as a near whisper. "I'm still prepared."

His arms tightened around her. He closed his eyes and rested his cheek against the top of her head. "Oh, Katherine...I want to make love to you so very much."

He held her closely for a moment longer, then brought his mouth against hers, filling her with his desire.

More than anything, she wanted Scott Blake to make love to her. She melted in his embrace, savored the texture of his tongue against hers, and quivered as his hands caressed her back and shoulders. Elation soared inside her as she returned all the heat of his fervor.

In one smooth motion, he scooped her up in his arms and carried her across the room toward the stairs. Her fingers went to the buttons on his shirt and unfastened them one by one. By the time they reached the top of the stairs, she had his shirt completely undone. He released her from his arms as he stood next to the bed, then gently cupped her face in his hands.

Katherine saw the smoldering intensity of his ardor in his eyes. Did she dare to hope that those eyes also contained love? His mouth captured hers again, his kiss hot and exciting.

He pulled his wallet from his pants pocket, took out the condom packets, and placed them on the nightstand. He answered her questioning look. "From Friday night when we went out to dinner…wishful thinking on my part, not an assumption."

Like some sort of dream sequence in a movie, they slowly and sensuously undressed each other, pieces of clothing dropping to the carpeting one at a time. He laid her back into the softness of the large bed, then stretched out next to her. His hand caressed the length of her body before finally coming to rest over the fullness of her breast.

"You are so beautiful, so exquisite. I want to please you so much." His words settled over her like a silken magic cloth.

The heat of his inflamed desire touched her bare skin with his lips and his fingers. He trailed sensual kisses across her cheek and down the side of her neck. She arched her back to press her body more fully against his. Her arms encircled him, her hands caressing his broad shoulders and strong back. His tongue swept over the sensitive skin between her breasts, then he kissed the underside of each one. He gently manipulated her nipples, teasing them to taut peaks.

Shivers of delight darted through her body. A soft moan escaped her lips as he drew her nipple into his mouth. He gently sucked as she ran her foot along his bare calf. Her breathing became more labored as his mouth demanded more. A skillful lover, he seemed to instinctively know each and every place to touch her, how to excite her senses to new heights of pleasure.

Katherine felt herself sinking into a mindless abyss. Nothing mattered except Scott and the wonderful things he did to her, the incredible sensations he created within her. She gave herself totally and completely, no doubt or reservations in her mind. As unlikely as she knew it to be, as preposterous a situation to exist from such a short acquaintance, she knew she loved him. She loved him so very much. She wanted to be with him always.

Scott caressed the gentle curve of her hip, teased the dark downy softness at the apex of her thighs. Her entire body pulsed as he slipped his hand along her smooth inner thigh. Her soft moans and whimpers of delight only added to the incendiary atmosphere sizzling around them like a hot desert day.

He rolled her over on top of him, her body soft and

supple, her skin silky. His fingers tickled down her back, then he caressed the roundness of her bare bottom. The swell of her firm breasts pressed against his hard chest as it heaved with his ragged breathing. She represented the embodiment of everything he had ever wanted, everything he had been searching for all these years. He wanted to consume her, to possess her, to be possessed by her, to be part of her for all time.

Her passionate response to him exceeded his expectations, so much more than he had hoped for. She filled his every waking moment. It shocked him to realize how quickly everything had happened. It had only been a week, but he felt as though he had known her a lifetime. What shocked him even more was the realization that he wanted it to be a lifetime.

He rolled her onto her back, then grabbed one of the condom packets off the nightstand, ripped it open, and rolled it on his solid erection. She trembled as he brushed his fingers through her downy triangle, then slipped a finger between the warm, moist folds of her femininity.

"Oh, Scott—" His mouth came down hard on hers, cutting off her words. He gave to her as much unbridled, frenzied passion as he demanded from her.

He inserted his knee between her thighs, gently spreading them wider. Poised above her, he slowly penetrated the heat of her body. He heard her quick gasp as he entered her. Her arms drew him closer. A delicious thrill surged between them as he thrust deeply.

They immediately fell into a slow, smooth rhythm. Her hips rose to meet his every stroke. They moved in sync, so attuned to each other. They achieved a rhythmic unison, a harmony of oneness as if they were longtime lovers. Each savored the sensual feelings, the growing tremors of excitement.

He captured her mouth, his tongue thrusting in coordination with the cadence of his hips. Her taste as sweet as the first time they had kissed, her lips as soft. His movements became more intense. The rapture built deep inside him.

Her cry of ecstasy enhanced the sensual way she locked her hips tightly against his. He reveled in every delicious sensation of her orgasmic contractions, an experience he wanted to repeat again and again. Forever.

Scott could not hold back any longer. With one final urgent thrust, his body stiffened, then he shuddered as the spasms overtook him. He buried his face in her neck, holding her tightly in his embrace. His breath came in hard puffs.

Their bodies glistened with a thin sheen of perspiration as they lay together in her bed. He placed a soft kiss on her cheek. Neither tried to speak. They held each other in silence as their breathing slowly returned to normal. He stroked her hair, smoothing back the loose tendrils that clung to her damp face, then brushed his lips softly against hers.

She remained in his arms. He delighted in her softness, cherished her closeness. He had never felt so at one with any woman. If only he could stay in her bed, stay with her. They basked in the golden afterglow of their intense lovemaking. They exchanged the murmurings of lovers as they sensually and playfully touched each other, laughed together, and tenderly held each other. It was a time of warmth and closeness combined with quiet reflection.

"Come away with me for the weekend. We'll find a romantic hideaway somewhere up the coast." Scott's words tickled Katherine's ear, causing shivers of excitement to race up her spine.

Never in her life had she felt the way she did at this very moment. Right now, he was the center of her universe. "You're forgetting the auction. The closer we get to it, the more work there is to do."

He frowned. "It's not this coming weekend, is it?"

"No, it's three weeks from yesterday, but things are starting to get hectic. This coming Friday night is the press conference, and after that, I'll be totally buried in the preparations for the event."

He kissed her on the cheek and gave her a teasing grin. "Then you'll need a break, need to go away for the weekend to replenish your energy, to relax before you wear yourself out and become totally exhausted."

She studied the honesty and openness covering his face, an expression that belied the smoldering intensity in his green eyes. "This coming weekend is out of the question." She paused, not sure whether her question would be appropriate. "Do I have another choice?"

He nibbled at her earlobe and teased the corners of her mouth. "How about the weekend after that, the one between the press conference and the auction?"

Her answer came out barely above a whisper as she traced the outline of his lips with her index finger. She knew she shouldn't take time off, that it was not the responsible thing to be doing at this time. She also knew it was what she wanted the most. "I'd like that. I'd like that very much."

****

Scott sat at his desk early Monday morning, eager to face whatever the day had to offer. He had stayed at Katherine's house until almost five o'clock in the morning, leaving only to go home to get ready for work. The memory of their lovemaking flooded his mind. It had been very special. She was a warm, responsive, caring woman with a passionate sensuality that could melt anything.

His reflections were interrupted by the buzzing of the intercom. "Yes, Amelia."

"Liz Torrance is on the phone. She wants to talk to you about the auction."

Liz and Scott talked for almost half an hour. He provided her with the information on the date package he had put together. They talked about convenient times for publicity pictures and interviews and set up a schedule agreeable to both of them. With the auction so near at hand, everyone at the charity involved in its preparations would be very busy.

As soon as he finished his conversation with Liz, he turned his attention to a new project that had just come in. He needed to study the architect's plans, spec out the materials required, and do a bid on a twenty-story building. The request had come from George Weddington. He was the architect who designed all the shopping centers for the Colgrave Corporation, not just the one in San Rafael. As with Brian Colgrave, Scott had a very close working relationship with George Weddington, one based on mutual respect and the desire to produce a quality product. He cleared his mind of all intruding thoughts and concentrated on this new bid.

****

Katherine, too, had a busy day planned—a fund-raising meeting in the morning and an auction-planning meeting in the afternoon. She paused in her thoughts long enough to allow a warm glow to envelop her. She had never felt so alive. Just the memory of her lovemaking with Scott made her body tingle. For the first time, she truly looked forward to the future and the excitement it held.

She grabbed three file folders off the top of her desk in her home office and shoved them into her attaché case. She turned to leave, then halted long enough to gather all the other files cluttering her desktop. With a quick sweep of her hand, she brushed them into a desk drawer, so they were out of sight.

As soon as Katherine arrived at the Hyatt, Liz showed her the list of all fifteen participating bachelors along with their date packages. It was the first hint she had of what Scott planned. He had refused to tell her. She read his date package report with keen interest.

He proposed a weekend in Yosemite National Park, about a four-hour drive from San Francisco. He had reserved two rooms at the luxurious Ahwahnee Hotel in Yosemite Valley for the weekend following the auction, the first weekend in November. He considered that an ideal time for the Valley. The summer crowds had gone, and it was too early for winter skiers. That weekend was usually the peak of fall color for the many deciduous trees. He stressed the nature and environmental aspects of the weekend, the assumption being that whoever bid on it would be someone who enjoyed the outdoors, walking the trails, communing with nature.

As Katherine floated through the finance meeting,

Jim Dalton made particular mention of how radiant she looked. They discussed budgets for the various projects and allocated funds for specific items. Following the finance committee meeting, they broke for lunch before the auction meeting that afternoon. Liz excused herself from lunch to take care of some personal errands. As she started to leave, the elevator doors opened.

"Lynn, over here." Katherine waved as soon as she saw Lynn step out of the elevator. She had asked Lynn to help with arrangements for the auction and the fund-raising party at her grandfather's house following the auction.

Lynn quickly crossed the lobby to where Katherine and Jim waited. "I hope I'm not late."

"Not at all." Katherine turned toward Jim. "Jim Dalton, I'd like to introduce Lynn Blake. Lynn is a former schoolteacher who was good enough to come out of retirement and accept our offer to work at the Oakland center with Cheryl. She also happens to be the mother of one of our bachelors." She turned toward Lynn. "Jim is a member of the finance committee and also on the board of directors. He's worked with us from the very beginning, and we couldn't get along without all of his—"

Jim's outgoing laugh cut into Katherine's words as he turned toward Lynn. "Yes, and next month I'm applying for sainthood." He extended his hand. "It's a pleasure to meet you, Lynn. Katherine has said many good things about you."

"The pleasure is all mine." Lynn returned his smile as they shook hands.

"Well, ladies, shall we grab some lunch?"

Katherine was very pleased with herself. She did

not believe in matchmaking. She had suffered the efforts of her friends and business associates for years, but she really felt Jim Dalton and Lynn Blake would have so much in common. When it was suggested that the committee could use another person to help with auction planning, she immediately offered Lynn's name. She had been very pleased when Lynn had agreed to take on the extra work.

Lunch turned out to be more fun than Katherine had anticipated. Lynn and Jim hit it off immediately. He regaled them with stories and anecdotes from the days he referred to as his *reckless youth*. Yes, indeed, Katherine was very pleased with herself.

The afternoon auction meeting was all business. Lynn contributed several good suggestions, and the committee accomplished quite a bit. Following the auction meeting, Katherine drove directly to the Oakland center. As soon as she stepped through the door, Jenny ran to her. She picked up the little girl who seemed to be looking around for something.

"What's the matter, Jenny?" She gave the child a kiss on the cheek and smoothed back her bouncing curls.

"I want Scott."

"He's not here. He has work to do." The child squirmed so much that Katherine finally had to put her down.

Cheryl watched them with a teasing twinkle in her eyes. "Jenny was telling us about your picnic."

The little girl giggled. "They were kissing."

Katherine *knew* her face had turned every shade of red known to man and nature plus some more, a situation not helped by the amused smiles of everyone at the center.

She watched as Jenny left the room. Then, in an attempt to change the subject as quickly as possible, she turned to Cheryl and spoke in a low, serious voice. "You are aware of what happened yesterday?"

Cheryl's manner became very professional. "Yes, I knew as soon as I saw Lynn arrive with Jenny that something was wrong. Sergeant Caswell called later this morning with the same information that Lynn gave me." She paused for a moment. "What happens now?"

"I guess…" Katherine's voice quavered. "I guess we need to find her a good home." Her face took on a look of determination. "I don't want her in and out of foster homes. I want her to have a real home and a real family who will give her the love she deserves."

Cheryl leveled a cool, appraising look at her. "How about your home?"

Katherine held her look for a long moment, then turned away without responding to her comment. Jenny needed more than just a place to live. She needed a home and a family, both a mother and father who would be there for her, a house with a yard where she could play on a swing, a bouncing little puppy, a…

****

Scott left his office following a busy day. He had stayed late working on the bid for George Weddington's office building. As he headed north across the Golden Gate Bridge, his mind turned to Katherine. She occupied more and more of his thoughts. If he wasn't occupied with a specific task, she automatically invaded his mind. On this particular occasion, his thoughts turned to their upcoming weekend out of town. He wanted it to be something very special.

Shock hit him when he pulled his car into the driveway and saw Billy sitting on his front porch. Billy jumped up and started for the car.

"Billy…what are you doing here?" Scott opened the car door and quickly got out.

"Uh…look, there's…" Billy was obviously uncomfortable.

All of Scott's senses were on immediate alert. Something was definitely wrong.

"Let's go inside." He unlocked the front door, and they entered the house. Billy followed him and immediately slumped into a chair.

Scott stared at him. "Okay. What's on your mind?"

"Well…you got some trouble at the construction site." Billy shifted uncomfortably in his chair, his gaze darting nervously around the room.

"What kind of trouble? You've only worked there two days, Friday and today. What do you know that I don't?"

Billy took immediate offense at Scott's words. "Hey, man. I know what I saw!" He glared at Scott but quickly calmed down.

"All right, tell me what you saw."

Billy rose and paced around the room, finally coming to rest on the deck overlooking the bay. "You got a nice view here. Kind of like your ol' la—I mean, your mom's."

"Thank you. Now, get to the point."

"Yeah. Well, uh, you got a couple of guys doin' drugs on the job."

Scott jerked to attention. He had always been very emphatic that anyone caught drinking on the job or doing drugs would be fired immediately—no exceptions, no warnings, and no second chances. Everyone who worked on his crews had been apprised of that long-standing rule and had to sign for a copy of the company's employment handbook that said the same thing. "Are you sure about this?"

Billy's anger flared again. "Yeah, I'm sure. They're also stealing stuff. Nothin' big…yet."

"Who else knows about this?"

"I ain't told no one, just you."

"Why didn't you tell John Barclay? He's in charge of the project, and he's on-site all the time."

"Hey, I don't know him from nobody. He could be part of it for all I know." Billy paused momentarily as if to collect his thoughts. This conversation was obviously very difficult for him, not part of the way he did things. He glared at Scott for a long moment, then spoke in a calmer, more controlled manner. "I ain't no snitch. They don't bother me, and I don't mess in their business, but they're stealin' from you and doing drugs. They could be hurtin' the job. You've been straight with me. I just wanted to return the favor." He headed for the door. "I gotta go."

"Wait a minute. Who is it? What are their names?"

"I said all I'm gonna say. If you trust this John guy, then let him figure it out. It shouldn't be too tough if he just keeps his eyes open." With that, Billy slammed out the front door and hurried down the street.

Scott sat in stunned silence for several minutes, then moved to the phone and called John Barclay. "And John, when we bust these guys, let's make sure we do it so that Billy has no involvement. Just tell them you've been on to them for a while and have been watching them. I know it's difficult to keep track of everything on a job this big, especially at the start when routines are still in the flexible stage, but first thing in the morning start a thorough inventory to determine exactly what's missing."

"Wouldn't that alert them to our suspicions? Maybe the inventory check should come from somewhere else, some place not directly connected to the day-to-day activities on site."

"You're right. That would be better. I'll have the inventory done by someone not connected with that project and claim it's part of an annual audit or maybe a requirement of the insurance company."

Having completed his business with John, Scott fixed dinner. As he ate, his thoughts turned again to Katherine and their upcoming weekend. He dialed her phone number but only got her voice mail. He wasn't surprised to find her not at home. He started to dial her cell phone but changed his mind. All the last-minute auction preparations were keeping her very busy. The charity business needed to take precedence over his personal desires.

****

Katherine spent the evening at her grandfather's house. She poured herself a glass of wine and one for her grandfather. "My heart just goes out to her, Grandpa. She's only three, and she's already been through more than some people go through in an entire lifetime. She needs a home and a family." She tried to suppress the sob that forced its way out and the tears that threatened. "Sometimes I just feel so helpless. I want so much for everything to be okay for her."

RJ Fairchild studied his granddaughter. "You

identify very closely with her, don't you?"

"Yes, I do. I don't want her to make the same mistakes I did. I don't want her to spend half her life wondering what she did to cause her mother not to love her. I don't want her to blame herself for her mother's death. I don't want her to have to wait until she's an adult before she understands and learns to deal with the reality of causes rather than just being controlled by the symptoms."

A quick surge of anguish darted through her. "I don't want her to be so desperate to have someone love her that she'll run off and marry the first person who pays even the slightest attention to her." *And then find out that all he ever wanted was a piece of the family fortune. That he was sleeping with anything in a skirt, including the person she thought was her best friend. That he flaunted his infidelities in public and would only agree to a quiet divorce without a scandal and the harsh glare of publicity if he was paid a huge cash settlement.*

A cold shiver ran up her spine as a tear trickled down her cheek. She would do everything she could to make sure Jenny was protected from all the emotional upheaval she had been subjected to as a child. She would make sure the little girl knew that someone loved her and cared about her.

It was late when Katherine arrived home. She checked her phone messages. Only one call. She immediately recognized Scott's voice and his teasing tone.

"This is an obscene phone call. Since you're not there to receive this call in person, I'll have to be content with some heavy breathing." She laughed out loud as she heard his exaggerated panting. "If you find any of this even mildly stimulating, call me at my office in the morning. We'll see if we can't do something obscene together tomorrow night. I'd even be willing to buy you dinner first." There was a brief pause, then she heard his words, soft and caring. "Good night, Katherine. I—" He never finished his sentence.

"Good night, Scott. I love you."

****

Katherine and Scott left the little Italian restaurant tucked away in a corner of the North Beach area. He slipped his arm around her shoulders as they walked toward the car. They enjoyed the comfort of their closeness. Neither felt pressured to talk, nor awkward with the silence.

She turned to him as he pulled his car into her driveway. "Would you like to come in for coffee?"

He ran his fingers across her cheek as his breathing quickened. "Did you really think you needed to ask?" He brushed his lips lightly against hers, then opened the car door. They walked hand in hand into the house.

As soon as they reached the kitchen, he pulled her into his embrace, his voice thick with emotion. "I don't really want any coffee."

Her response was a mere whisper. "Neither do I."

He took her hand and led her up the stairs to the third floor. They paused next to her bed. He cupped her face in his hands and studied her for a long moment. "I've never met anyone like you. I didn't think anyone like you even existed." He lowered his mouth to hers, infusing her with his deep feelings and emotions.

****

Early Wednesday morning, Scott flew to Los

Angeles for a series of meetings. He told Katherine he wouldn't be home until late Thursday night, and they would have dinner Friday. Katherine spent Wednesday and Thursday working on the publicity campaign for the bachelor auction. The publicity releases went out, and a press conference was scheduled for Friday afternoon.

On Thursday morning, she appeared in court with Billy and Bob Townsend. As Bob had predicted, with the circumstances surrounding the incident and a deposition from John Barclay about Billy's good work record, the judge gave Billy three months' probation. The entire situation remained part of his juvenile record to be sealed when he turned eighteen. Everything seemed to be progressing in a smooth manner.

Friday morning found Scott at the construction site in San Rafael. He spent half an hour with John Barclay in the construction office trailer. After their conversation Monday night, John had kept a watchful eye on all the crew members, especially those working in areas in proximity to where Billy worked. By early Tuesday afternoon, he had spotted the two culprits working in an area fairly isolated from the rest of the crew. He kept a log of their activities. They appeared to be doing cocaine a couple of times a day. On Wednesday morning, a team of *auditors* showed up and began a thorough inventory.

Scott and John left the office trailer and walked briskly across the construction site. With few amenities and no pleasantries, Scott immediately dismissed the two workers. In accordance with company policy, he presented them with a written notice of termination stating specifically why they were being fired without notice. Their final checks had already been drawn. Before the checks were handed over, the two men were required to countersign the personnel form stating that they had been presented with full documentation as to why they had been dismissed.

"Our attorneys will contact the police and provide them full details, with the possibility of criminal charges pending the outcome of the inventory." With those final words, Scott had security escort the two men from the site. He could tell from the looks on the men's faces that they were shaken to their boots. They would not be back looking for revenge. In fact, he assumed they would probably leave the state immediately before criminal charges could be filed.

John walked Scott to his car, giving Scott an opportunity to ask him how Billy was working out. John was thoughtful for a moment before answering. "He works hard, keeps to himself, doesn't give anyone any problems. There's one thing, though. Every day at lunch, he disappears but is always back on time. On his first day here, he asked around for anyone who could give him a lift as far as Tiburon each afternoon at the end of the workday."

Chapter Eight

Scott stopped by his house on the way from the construction site to his office. He needed to change for the auction press conference since he wouldn't have time to return home that afternoon. His mind turned to Katherine again. After the press conference, they would go out to dinner. He had not seen her since he had left her house about midnight Tuesday. A frown tugged at his forehead as he drove south across the Golden Gate Bridge into San Francisco. He missed her, and it bothered him how much he missed her, considering he had only been out of town for two days.

The press conference took place at the Hyatt Regency. Katherine stayed in the background while Liz presided over the activities as she would with the auction, too. The number of reporters and photographers present surprised him. He had no idea something like this would attract so much publicity. He felt uncomfortable, ill at ease with the cameras and questions directed specifically to him. He disliked being on display.

One reporter in particular irritated him by asking about his personal relationship with Katherine, noting that they had been seen dining together in an atmosphere that was far from businesslike. He tactfully provided one of those *nonanswer* type of answers.

He loosened his tie as he and Katherine walked out

of the hotel. "I'm sure glad that's over. I don't know how you deal with that constant glare of publicity, having your life continually held up to public scrutiny."

A sigh escaped Katherine's lips. "You get used to it after a while. You just have to learn not to let it control you, that's all."

Her mind flashed back to the press conference. She could tell from watching Scott how uncomfortable he was, particularly when the questions had centered on their relationship. She wondered for a moment if the public spotlight would eventually cause problems between them and shivered at the thought.

They claimed their own cars from valet parking. Scott followed Katherine home so she could leave her car, then they went to dinner. He had selected a charming French restaurant off the beaten path. They spent an enchanting two hours at the restaurant, mesmerized by the warm glow of growing yet unspoken love that surrounded them.

Katherine had never been so happy, truly happy, in her entire life as she was whenever they were together.

"Do you have any plans for tomorrow?" Scott clasped her hand as they walked to the car.

"I promised Jenny I'd take her to the zoo. Would you like to go with us?"

"Very much so."

The next day, the weather turned cool in spite of the sunshine. Katherine helped Jenny with her jacket as Scott pulled into the parking lot. The little girl was so excited she had hardly been able to sit still. She kept up a constant line of chatter from the moment they picked her up at the center.

Jenny's eyes widened with wonder and awe as she

craned her neck to look up at the giraffes. She giggled and clapped her hands at the antics of the monkeys. She kept repeating *big kitty, big kitty* when she saw the lions. Everything seemed so fresh and new as seen through her eyes.

They returned to Katherine's house that evening. It had been a very busy day for the little girl. She tucked Jenny into bed in the guest room, then joined Scott in the den. "She went right to sleep. She was exhausted."

Scott flashed a decidedly lascivious grin. "How about tucking me into bed? Of course, I must warn you. I don't think I'll be going right to sleep. I'm not exhausted...yet."

She tried to suppress the grin tugging at the corners of her mouth as she snuggled next to him on the couch. A warm glow radiated throughout her body when he slipped his arm around her shoulders and drew her closer. She covered his hand with hers and leaned her head against his shoulder.

They stayed together on the couch, enjoying the quiet moment. Neither spoke, just being together was enough. Occasionally, Scott would lean over and place a soft kiss on her cheek or forehead.

"Mommy...mommy..."

Jenny's screams pierced the quiet of the house. Katherine jumped to her feet and raced to the guest room. The little girl had experienced another of her nightmares.

"Jenny, it's okay. I'm here with you." She wrapped the sobbing child in her arms and rocked her gently, assuming she would go right back to sleep.

Between sobs, Jenny asked the question for the first time, the question Katherine knew she would eventually have to answer. "Where's my mommy?"

A hard lump formed in Katherine's throat, and her mouth went dry. She had been dreading this moment, dreading the time when she would have to tell Jenny what had happened. Cheryl had volunteered to be the one to do it. As a child psychologist, she would have been better qualified to handle the situation, but Katherine felt a strong responsibility to be the one dealing with the crisis. She wiped the tears from Jenny's cheeks and smoothed back her blonde curls. Big brown eyes...innocent and frightened eyes...looked up at her.

"Jenny, honey...your mommy..." She desperately tried to remember exactly how her grandfather had told her about her own mother. She had asked her father, but he had not known what to say. So the task fell to her grandfather who had taken the responsibility. Her grandfather who, once again, had been her strength and lifeline. She didn't know how much the little girl would understand, but she had to try.

She hugged the child tightly against her body. "Your mommy has gone away and won't be coming back." She carefully measured her words. "It's not because she doesn't want to come back. It's because she can't come back. Your mommy... Your mommy was in an accident. She was hurt really badly, then she...she..." The words caught in her throat. She had to force them out. "She died."

She continued to hug the child closely to her. "Your mommy wanted to come back. She wanted to be with you again. Your mommy loved you. Always remember that. Your mommy loved you, and she couldn't help that she had to go away." She continued to rock the little girl gently in her arms. "I know what you're going through, Jenny. I know exactly. I know about the bad dreams. I know how frightening they are for you. They're just like the dreams I used to have." She took a steadying breath, then continued talking, as much to herself as to the child.

"It's not your fault, Jenny. It's not your fault that your mommy went away, and it's not your fault that she won't be able to come back. You didn't do anything wrong." She looked into the innocent little face. "Do you understand that, my precious? You did not do anything wrong. It is not your fault. I love you, Jenny, and I won't let anything or anyone ever hurt you again. I'll always be here whenever you need me. Please believe me, I know exactly what you're feeling and what's happening to you. I know you don't really understand now, because you're too young, but someday you will. Then everything will be okay." She hugged Jenny securely against her body as tears trickled down her cheeks, tears shed not for her own memories but for the uncertainty of Jenny's future.

****

Scott stood back from the bedroom door. He listened to Katherine's words and felt the emotion behind them, another piece of the puzzle that seemed to surround her life. He had been left with the distinct impression that she was talking about herself as much as she had been talking to Jenny. He recognized it as an important moment for Katherine and Jenny to be sharing. Even though he wanted to provide comfort to both of them, he would not interfere. He quietly returned to the den to wait.

He thought back to their excursion to the zoo.

Katherine had seemed as excited as Jenny. As he had watched them together, a warm feeling of contentment settled deep inside him. With Katherine at his side and the darling little girl discovering wondrous new things, he felt the missing pieces of his life had been found.

****

The weekend had gone by very quickly, too quickly for Scott. He settled in at his desk. Amelia brought him a cup of coffee and the morning mail. There used to be time for everything, but not anymore. He stared at the computer monitor as he scrolled through his schedule. The coming weekend, he and Katherine were going to a romantic hideaway, the following weekend was the bachelor auction, and the week after that, his date package in Yosemite. And interspersed with those personal activities were numerous business meetings and an increasingly heavy workload.

He turned his mind to business. The first item for that Monday morning was a revision of the bid on George Weddington's latest project. He unrolled the new blueprints and began studying them, comparing them with the old ones. It looked to be a long workday.

He finally arrived home late that evening. As soon as he entered the house, he noticed the envelope on the floor, obviously shoved under the door—the envelope that had contained Billy's paycheck. Inside it, he found three crisp new twenty-dollar bills, nothing else. Scott smiled as he pocketed the money. The crew had been paid that morning. Billy must have gone to the bank on his lunch break.

Even though it was late, he placed a call to Katherine. He wanted to hear her voice before going to bed.

"I didn't wake you, did I? I just got home and wanted to say good night before going to bed."

"You're just now getting home from work?" Her surprise traveled through the airways. "You've certainly had a long day."

"George Weddington sent over some revised plans for the office building, so I needed to do a revised bid for the project on top of the normal day's workload. How about you? I assume your day was filled with auction plans."

"I don't want to call it chaos, because that would sound like we weren't organized." She emitted a soft chuckle. "But it was somewhat chaotic, especially needing to make sure my schedule is clear for this weekend. And speaking of this weekend, where are we going?"

"I guess you'll find out when we get there," he teased.

"But I need to know so I can pack the appropriate clothes."

"It's only a weekend, and I can assure you we won't be attending any formal events. Just casual and relaxing."

"That's all you're going to tell me?"

"Ah, Ms. Fairchild, that's one of the things I admire about you...that ability to immediately grasp the situation." He laughed. "You're right. That's all I'm going to tell you."

****

The balance of the week proved very hectic for each of them. They could not get their schedules to mesh. She had two dinner meetings on nights when he was clear. He had a meeting on the only open night on her schedule. They managed a quick lunch together, the only time they saw each other. They talked on the phone each night, even if only for a few minutes.

Friday finally arrived. Scott picked Katherine up that afternoon. As soon as he stepped into her house, he pulled her into his arms. "It seems like forever since I've seen you. Last weekend went too fast, and this week has gone too slowly." Without giving her a chance to say anything, he captured her mouth with his, filling her with his longing and desire.

Katherine trembled in his embrace as she willingly returned every emotion, every heated promise of what their weekend would hold. She had told her grandfather she wasn't looking for a husband, but more and more her thoughts turned toward marriage and a family.

Cheryl had been right. Jenny belonged in her home, but not just the two of them. Scott provided the missing ingredient, the person who would allow them to be a real family. She wished she knew for sure how he felt. He said all the right things, but he had never told her he loved her. She more than merely wanted him. She *needed* him. She and Jenny both needed him as a permanent part of their lives.

"Are you ready to go?"

His question interrupted her thoughts. "Absolutely."

She reached for her weekend bag, but he took it before she could pick it up. A few minutes later, he headed the car north, then cut across to the coast. He had picked a charming inn at the Russian River as their final destination. Their spacious room included a wood-burning fireplace and large deck with a breathtaking view of the spectacular coastline. An ice bucket and bottle of champagne had been placed in their room, per his instructions.

They stood on the deck overlooking the ocean. He held her hand as the sounds of the crashing surf filled their ears with the majesty of nature. "This is beautiful, Scott, but I feel very guilty. I should be home working on charity business. It's not just the auction. There's also the fund-raising party afterward and the fund-raising campaign for the upcoming year. There's so much work to do yet."

He put his fingertips to her lips, silencing her words. "This weekend is for us." He brushed his lips lightly against hers. "No one is allowed to discuss business or work."

They went inside. He immediately started a fire in the fireplace, then uncorked the champagne. With the flames casting soft, flickering shadows across the room, they clinked glasses and wordlessly toasted each other. Their eyes locked in an emotional moment that neither could deny. They sipped their champagne and allowed the warm closeness that existed to settle around them.

After enjoying the quiet time together, they went to the dining room. Dinner was a leisurely affair filled with casual conversation, yet the underlying current of sensuality that flowed swiftly and insistently kept surfacing. The weekend had started on a perfect note. There would be no distractions. Nothing to dampen their enjoyment, nothing to inhibit their quest to learn as much about each other as possible.

Nothing to interfere with their growing love.

Katherine lay nestled in Scott's arms, her head resting against his shoulder and her hand on his chest.

Things were so perfect. She had never been happier. She felt his chest rise and fall with the slow even breathing that indicated he had fallen asleep.

A smile curled the corners of her mouth as she snuggled closer to him and closed her eyes. They had the entire weekend ahead of them. He would not have to get up in the middle of the night or early in the morning to go home. They would wake up together, as they should. A contented sigh escaped her lips before she, too, slipped into a warm sleep.

****

Saturday turned out to be everything she hoped it would be. After breakfast, Scott rented bicycles, and they rode down quiet country lanes. That afternoon they walked hand in hand along the nearly deserted beach, pausing to pick up seashells along the way—a time of closeness and contentment. That night after dinner, Scott lit a fire in the fireplace. They sat on the floor, watching the flames. Neither spoke, they simply enjoyed being together. So in tune with each other, so in sync. Katherine wanted the feeling to last forever.

It was late when they finally went to bed. They made love slowly and sensuously, rather than with the heated frenzy that had gripped them in the shower that morning. Time had no meaning. They had forever to be together. Every minute of the day her love for him grew stronger and stronger. They finally succumbed to blissful sleep.

They slept in Sunday morning. When they woke, they continued to lie in bed, talking softly and savoring the leisurely feeling of not having to get up.

"How is Billy doing on his job? I haven't heard anything since the day we were in court. Since I'm responsible for him, I thought I'd better ask."

"He seems to be doing okay. John says he's always on time, doesn't cause any trouble, and does the work assigned to him. In fact, he went one step further. I know it was entirely against his nature to tell on someone, so to speak, but he exposed a situation at the construction site that involved a couple the crew members who were doing drugs on the job and stealing. Because of him we were able to take care of the matter before it got completely out of hand and do it in such a manner that no one suspected Billy had any involvement." An involuntary frown wrinkled his forehead. "The only thing that bothers me is why he asked around for a ride to Tiburon each night after work and what he was doing at Mom's house the Saturday we went on our picnic. She said he was helping her with something, but he looked too guilty for it to be that simple."

Katherine's brow furrowed in thought. "You know, when I arrived back at the center the day we went sailing, he was gone. Cheryl didn't know where he was, and Lynn was also gone. When she came back, she said Billy was running some errands for her." She looked quizzically at Scott. "The two of them are up to something. I wonder what's going on."

She brightened as if struck by a sudden thought. "I saw the paperwork on your date package for the auction. Some lucky lady is going to have a very nice weekend. Yosemite Valley is beautiful that time of year. The big-leaf maples are bright yellow, the oaks have turned golden, and the dogwoods are a brilliant red. An added plus is that the park is usually uncrowded that time of year…at least uncrowded by Yosemite

Valley standards."

"I don't suppose you'd like to bid on me? Keep me from being embarrassed when no one wants to bid on me?" He shot her a mischievous grin.

"I don't think no one bidding on you will be a problem. I think the problem will be a bidding war as the ladies fight over you." Her amusement at his apprehension was obvious. "Anyway, this coming Saturday night will tell us for sure."

"I'm going to feel guilty about running off for the weekend with another woman."

"I'll tell you what. You can make it up to me. The family lodge at Lake Tahoe is available between Christmas and New Year's Day. We can go there and hide away from the rest of the world."

"What would you like to do today?" He placed a loving kiss of her forehead. "We have until early afternoon before we need to head back to reality."

A soft chuckle escaped her throat. "Reality… Wouldn't it be nice if this was reality?"

"I suppose it's not practical to try to make this a day-to-day reality, but we can certainly take this feeling of contentment home with us."

A feeling of contentment, something she had never truly had before she met Scott. Katherine wanted to tell him about her past, share with him her most intimate and painful secrets, confide things no living person outside of her family and the family attorney knew, bare her deepest inner recesses. She wanted to tell him more than what she already had about having been married for a brief time. She wanted him to know everything about her marriage and how much Jerry's callous, uncaring actions had hurt her even before his demands for money. She wanted to tell him about her painful childhood, about the beatings, her mother's eventual suicide, and her own subsequent feelings of extreme guilt.

She wanted him to know everything, but she hesitated. For some reason unknown even to herself, she couldn't tell him. It bothered her that she could not let go of this last remaining vestige of the ordeal that had haunted her youth. Perhaps it was because of Jenny. She could not allow herself release from the last remaining hurdle to her own complete happiness until she knew Jenny had a good home. She truly loved the little girl. An involuntary shiver moved through her body.

"Are you cold?" He put his arms around her, pulling her to him and sharing the warmth of his body.

"I guess a little, yes." She snuggled closer to him. Another tremor of apprehension and anxiety shook her body. If only she knew how he really felt about her. Did he love her? Could he possibly love her as much as she loved him? Her euphoria became tinged with sadness and uncertainty. Hopefully, he wouldn't notice. She didn't want to spoil what had been a perfect weekend together. She placed a soft kiss on his chest.

He tickled his fingers across her hip, then seductively ran his hand across her bare bottom. In a voice quickly becoming thick with emotion, he whispered in her ear, "If we don't get up and get dressed very soon, I'm going to be forced to make love to you again."

"And that would be such a terrible thing because…" She rubbed her hand against his growing arousal. "You're turning me into a wanton, brazen woman."

A teasing grin came to his lips. "And that would be such a terrible thing because…" He cupped the fullness of her firm breast, his tongue quickly teasing her nipple to a taut point.

****

They packed, checked out, then went to the dining room. After lunch, they drove inland, following the river until they came to a grove of redwood trees. He parked the car in a roadside turnout. They walked along the trail, immersing themselves in the sights, sounds, and smells of the forest. When they stopped walking, they heard only the sounds of the birds, the breeze rustling through the treetops, the occasional cone dropping from a tree branch and hitting the ground with a plopping sound. For a brief moment, it seemed to Katherine that they must surely be the only people in the world, isolated from all the ills that had plagued mankind through the ages.

Scott pulled her into his embrace, brushed a loose tendril of hair from her cheek, and looked into the depths of her eyes. He placed a soft kiss on her lips.

She slipped her arms around his waist as she rested her head against his chest. "Thank you for this weekend. It's been the nicest time I've ever spent anywhere. I'm sorry it has to end."

"Thank you for sharing it with me…and it's not over yet. There's one more thing when we get back to town."

She looked at him questioningly. "More? What else could there be? Everything has already been so perfect."

He smiled at her like a little boy with a secret he

was having trouble keeping to himself. "You'll see." He clasped her hand in his, and they continued walking.

Scott felt the same nervousness he had experienced the previous Thursday when he went to the jewelry store to pick out the ring. The decision had been very difficult for him. Should he ask her to marry him first, then pick out the ring with her? Should he demonstrate his sincere intentions by already having the ring? He had been at a loss about how to buy a piece of jewelry for someone of vast wealth who could afford to buy herself the very best.

The one thing he did know for sure, the one absolutely positive fact, was how much he loved Katherine Fairchild, how much he wanted to spend the rest of his life with her. And that meant marriage, nothing less. He would tell her of his love and ask her to marry him when they got home.

****

They didn't arrive at Katherine's house until well after dark. Scott knew she would be very busy the entire week because of the auction. This would probably be their last opportunity to spend a significant amount of time alone together. He carried her suitcase up to her bedroom.

"Do you have a schedule showing the sequence of events for the auction?" He set her suitcase on her bed.

"Yes, in my office. There's a file folder in the desk drawer. Why don't you get that while I fix us a bite to eat?" She brushed her lips lightly against his, then disappeared down the stairs. He went into her office and opened the desk drawer.

Fifteen minutes passed with Scott still in her office, a file holder in his hand.

Her voice came from the bottom of the stairs as she called up to him. "Scott? Are you finding what you need?"

Scott forced himself to move, slowly descending the stairs as the overwhelming emotional pain flowed through him. "Yes, Ms. Fairchild. I believe I've found...*everything*." He held a file folder, the name Scott Blake printed on the tab in large block letters. "In fact"—he fought to keep the emotion out of his voice—"I believe I've found more than you intended...and definitely more than I expected to find."

Chapter Nine

"It's not what you think—"

"No?" Scott cut Katherine off in mid-sentence as he held up the folder. "It seems self-explanatory to me. You had me investigated. Perhaps to make sure I'm acceptable enough to associate with one of the elite Fairchilds?" He softened his voice, but the pain continued to churn in his gut. "It's a very thorough report. Whoever does your work is quite good. A personal financial statement, a financial statement for the company, my college records, a background check on my parents, and an in-depth background check on me. And all this in a report dated only two days after we met."

He emitted a heavy sigh of disillusionment. "Obviously, I didn't need to tell you that I had once been engaged." He flipped open the file and read an entry he found particularly detestable. " 'Numerous affairs handled in a discreet manner, none of them very serious. Applied for a marriage license five years ago, about the time his father died but never married. Unknown if there's any connection between the broken engagement and his father's death or if the timing of the two was coincidental.' You've left no stone unturned. The only thing missing is the name of my first pet."

Her eyes brimmed with tears. Her body visibly shook. "Scott, please listen—"

"The games of the socially elite…well, you win the trophy. I fell for it all the way. The only consolation is that things ended before I made a complete fool of myself by doing something—" His voice cracked as the words choked in his throat. "Like telling you how much I love you, asking you to marry me, and share my life."

He quickly recovered his composure. "Next time, I'll know to stay away from the society pages of the newspaper. The air is too rarified in your circle of reality. It prevents me from thinking clearly. Goodbye, Ms. Fairchild." He dropped the file folder on the table and walked out the door without looking back, his gut wrenching into a thousand knots.

There had been only one time in his entire life when he had felt as lost and distraught as he did at that moment. It was when his father had suddenly died. He thought nothing could ever again be that devastating.

He had been wrong.

He loved Katherine so much more than he had ever loved Angelina. In fact, at the time of the breakup of his engagement, he wondered if he had ever truly loved her at all. It was more a feeling of relief that it was over than anything else. There was no comparison between that and how he felt about Katherine. He got in his car and drove home, his mind completely oblivious to anything and everything going on around him.

Scott walked into his bedroom, not bothering to turn on the light, and thrust his hand into his jacket pocket. He withdrew a small velvet box, opened it, and removed the exquisite diamond ring. His hand closed around the ring, then he clutched it to his heart. He would never love anyone as much as he loved Katherine. He closed his eyes, trying desperately to make the pain go away. He had never known the depth of heartbreak he experienced at that moment.

****

As soon as Scott left her house, Katherine sank onto a kitchen chair—her body and mind numb, her reality a blank. She didn't know what to do. She only knew she wanted to hide away and never come out. How could life be at the very highest peak, then crash to the lowest depths fifteen minutes later? She stood up and slowly climbed the stairs to her bedroom. She could never love another man as much as she loved Scott. She collapsed across the bed, sobbing uncontrollably.

She cried herself to sleep, crying until she had no more tears. She spent a terrible night vacillating between utter despair, anger, and stubborn determination. The next morning, in the clear light of dawn, she began to pull herself together.

Despair gave way to the anger. Anger at herself for not having destroyed the report immediately rather than carelessly tossing it on her desk. Anger for allowing Scott to leave her house without insisting he listen to an explanation. Anger at her grandfather for having had Scott investigated in the first place. But mostly anger at Scott for not giving her a chance to explain.

His words kept coming back to her, words telling her he loved her, that he wanted to ask her to marry him. She knew in her heart that the words had come from his heart, that they had been his true feelings. How could he set aside the love that existed between them? To allow his wounded ego to prevail?

The anger spawned her stubborn determination. She had once told him she always got what she went after. She would show him the truth of that statement, that it wasn't just empty words. She loved him more than life itself. She would not allow that love to fall by the wayside.

Curl up and die may have been the way she felt last night, but today, fighting mad best described her mood. Scott Blake had more than met his match. She knew about hurt and rejection. She had learned through painful experience that she couldn't run and hide. She had to stand up and fight for what she wanted. If she did not succeed in getting through to him by Friday afternoon using Plan A, then she would put Plan B into service. One way or the other, she would make him listen to what she had to say.

****

Scott spoke into the intercom. "Tell Ms. Fairchild I'm not in. In fact, you can tell her I left the country, and you don't know when I'll be returning." He glared at the phone. What did she think she was trying to prove by calling him at work? There was nothing left to say. That report had said it all.

He had considered canceling out of the auction, but all the publicity had already been released. It would not be fair to the charity to leave them in a bind at the last minute. He would just have to make sure he kept clear of her that evening. After Saturday, he would put this entire episode behind him and get on with his life.

Time refused to move for Scott. Monday dragged by very slowly. It would seem that hours had passed, but when he glanced at his watch, he would find it had only been ten minutes. He could not concentrate. Finally he turned off his desk lamp and walked out into Amelia's office. "I'm calling it a day. I'll see you in the morning."

He refused to look directly at her. He knew he would only see her disapproval.

As Scott walked out of Amelia's office into the outside reception area, he spotted Katherine stepping out of the elevator. He quickly turned around and retraced his steps. As he passed Amelia's desk, he hurriedly whispered, "I'm not in to Ms. Fairchild. I'll be leaving by my private entrance."

He rushed into his office, closing the door behind him.

Katherine walked past the front receptionist and directly into Amelia's office. She tried to project a calm and controlled persona. She extended her most gracious smile as she approached the desk. "Good afternoon, Amelia. I'd like to see Scott. And please don't tell me that he's out of the country."

Amelia's gaze traveled nervously around the room, unable to look Katherine in the eye. "He's already gone for the day, Ms. Fairchild."

Katherine looked directly at Amelia. "His car is still in his parking space." She took a seat across the office. "I'll just wait, if you don't mind."

Amelia looked up at her. "You're welcome to wait if you'd like, but he really has gone for the day." The sadness in Amelia's eyes was so obvious, Katherine knew she told the truth.

****

To say it had been a lousy week would be a gross understatement. Scott sank into his chair and swiveled around until he could see out his office window. The low gray clouds threatened rain. The mist obscured the top of the towers on the Golden Gate Bridge, and the wind kicked up whitecaps on the bay. A perfect day. It exactly fit his mood. He stared blankly out the window, looking without really seeing.

He spun back around, opened his desk drawer, and withdrew the small velvet box. His intention had been to return it to the jeweler first thing Monday morning. He opened the box and took out the ring. For some reason, by some force beyond his conscious control, he had not been able to do it. Perhaps he wanted to keep one small piece of what had been some of the happiest days of his life. He turned the ring over in his fingers, allowing the diamonds to sparkle in the light before returning it to the box and placing the box back in his desk drawer.

Amelia entered his office carrying an arrangement of flowers. "Where would you like these? They just arrived."

"From Ms. Fairchild again? How many does that make this week? One a day Monday through Thursday and two of them today—six flower arrangements." He sighed heavily. "Do the same thing you did with the others. Send them to the hospital. Let someone enjoy them."

"Do you want to read the card?"

"Does it say anything different than the others?"

"No, Mr. Blake. It's the same as the others. 'We have to sit down and talk. Please come to my house at eight o'clock tonight.'"

He knew something needed to be done and soon. His state of mind had started to have a negative impact on the smooth running of the company—forgetting some things and dismissing others as not important to the moment. His mind refused to settle on business.

****

Katherine's week hadn't fared any better. As soon as she had concluded the Friday afternoon meeting with the banquet manager at the hotel to go over last-minute details, she stopped by the center to pick up Jenny. She was having an early dinner with her grandfather but wanted to be home by eight. Her grandfather had specifically requested that she bring the little girl. It warmed her heart to see the way he doted on the child, the same type of loving attention he had given her during those dark lonely years of her childhood. It was almost as though Jenny were the great-granddaughter he kept pestering Katherine to provide him. He had been right. She identified so closely with Jenny and her situation.

When she arrived at her grandfather's house with Jenny, she tried to put up a good front. Despite her earnest attempt, he immediately saw through her and recognized her distraught condition. Fortunately, he had not been given an opportunity to ask her about it. Jenny had immediately climbed onto his lap, giggled, and patted his cheek and nose.

As soon as Jenny fell asleep on the den couch following dinner, he approached Katherine. "What's wrong? You look miserable. I know the auction takes a lot of your energy, and you're always a basket case the night before because you're sure everything will blow up, but this is different."

She averted her gaze, not wanting to make eye contact with him. He was capable of getting any secret out of her, including the darkest and deepest secret of her entire life. "There's nothing wrong, Grandpa. It's like you said. The auction always has me uptight the night before. I'll be fine as soon as it's over."

His eyes narrowed as he studied her. "Katherine Sutton Fairchild, don't you dare lie to me. I can read you like a book."

She jerked to attention. It had been years since he addressed her by her full name. It was the same manner and tone he'd used to persuade her to tell him about her mother and about the beatings. Suddenly she felt like that frightened little girl again, knowing she could never tell anyone but unable to keep the pain inside any longer. She couldn't hold back her tears.

"It's Scott, Grandpa...I love him so much. How could things be so awful?" In an anguish-filled voice, she told him everything that had happened. "And I know he loves me, Grandpa. I know he does. He's just had his pride hurt and now..."

The old man comforted her, a thoughtful look on his face. "Well, Katherine. It seems I might have a small amount of culpability in the matter. Perhaps I'd—"

"Don't you dare do anything. It would only make matters worse. I've got to take care of this myself. If you interfere, Scott will feel like he's being manipulated even more than he already does. Please, Grandpa, don't interfere. Promise me."

"Okay, I promise." It obviously pained him greatly to see her so upset. Given the dynamic, take-charge type of person he was, his frustration at having his hands tied like that couldn't be hidden.

****

Saturday morning found Katherine very busy. The auction would begin at seven that night, and it seemed as if thousands of last-minute details still needed to be handled. Everyone's help had been enlisted. Even Billy pitched in. By three o'clock, things were as ready as they were going to be. Katherine and Liz went over their lists one more time, just to make sure. Lynn double-checked the mailing list and acceptances of the invited guests to the fund-raising party at RJ's mansion following the auction in the hotel ballroom.

"Could I have everyone's attention?" Katherine's voice rang out loud and clear across the ballroom. "I want to take a few minutes to thank all of you for the hard work you've put in to make this year's auction a rousing success. I think this will be the best one yet."

A round of applause greeted her comments.

"There will be the traditional invitation-only after-auction party at my grandfather's house. Make sure you have a printed invitation before leaving this afternoon. They will be collected at the door upon arrival at the party. One more thing. When I start pestering the guests for donations, you're allowed to ignore me." This statement was greeted with laughter and more applause. "You have already contributed more than enough. Again, thank you very much. Now, it's time to go home and put on your finest. We'll meet back here at six. Our bachelors are due at six-thirty, and at seven o'clock, we'll kick off our fund-raising campaign."

"I ain't so sure about this." Billy caught the disapproving look in Lynn's eyes as they walked out the door of the ballroom, headed toward her car. "Yeah, yeah, I know. *Ain't* ain't a word."

"Don't worry, you'll do just fine." She offered him her best confidence-inducing smile.

****

Scott was having trouble with the black tie. He disliked wearing a tux and really hated wrestling with the tie. On the fourth attempt, he finally managed to tie it so it looked right. He checked his appearance one last time in the full-length mirror.

He picked up the invitation to the party and stared at it. Well, that was one event he certainly had no intention of attending. He stared at it a moment longer, then stuck it in his jacket pocket. He would bring it along, just in case he got trapped into something. The evening could not be over soon enough to suit him. His stomach churned. The one thing he dreaded most—more than being put on public display, more than this stupid auction idea—was running into Katherine.

His entire reality ached. The week had been pure torture. She seemed to be everywhere, constantly in his mind—her sparkling turquoise eyes, beautiful face, dazzling smile, and her laugh. The way her body nestled warmly in his arms as she slept. That hauntingly sad expression he'd caught just a glimpse of when she comforted Jenny after the little girl's nightmare and the emotional words she had spoken while explaining to Jenny about why her mother would not be coming back, about how it wasn't Jenny's fault. Would the love he felt for Katherine ever fade? Would he ever be released from her spell? He closed his eyes and tried to compose himself.

****

Billy fidgeted as he got out of Lynn's car. It was the first time he had ever worn a suit and tie. It felt very awkward and uncomfortable. His new shoes felt funny, too. "Jeez, I can't do this!"

"You look very nice, Billy. Now, we're going to enjoy the evening's proceedings, then we're going to the party afterward. I think that would be a good time to make our announcement, don't you?"

"Announcement!" Billy's expression clearly showed borderline panic. "Come on, I agreed to doin' all this, but—"

"Calm down. You know very well you wouldn't have done it if you hadn't wanted to. All you needed was a little help to get started. You should be very proud of yourself. I'm very proud of you, and I know Katherine will be very proud, too. Now, let's go inside."

He eyed her intently for a moment. "What about Scott? Does he know?"

"I promised it would be our secret, that I wouldn't tell anyone what you were doing, and I haven't. Not even Scott." Lynn steered an obviously nervous Billy toward the hotel ballroom.

****

Katherine was dealing with her own pre-auction anxieties. She was a nervous wreck. She had neither seen nor talked to Scott since that horrible moment the previous Sunday night when she allowed him to walk out her door. She had been thankful for the last-minute frenzied activity surrounding the auction. It had kept her busy, leaving her very little time to reflect on her despair. But her nights had been spent in turmoil with not even one decent night's sleep. She knew everyone had been speculating behind her back about what had happened. She did not know what Lynn knew or suspected or what Scott might have told her.

And there was Jenny. She kept asking for Scott, and Katherine didn't know what to tell her. An overwhelming sadness enveloped Katherine, but she didn't know if it was for Jenny or for herself. A shudder moved through her body as she turned toward her closet. She needed to hurry. She didn't want to be late.

When she finally made it to the event, she moved quickly from group to group, talking to everyone for only a few minutes. When she saw Lynn and Billy, she immediately rushed toward them. "Billy, don't you look nice in your suit and tie. This is a new look for you. Is it something we're going to be seeing more often?"

He gazed at the floor, obviously embarrassed. "Yeah, well sorta...yeah. I didn't have nothin'—" He glanced at Lynn, then corrected his grammar. "I didn't have *anything* proper to wear this evening, so I bought a suit and this tie." His gaze nervously darted between Lynn and Katherine, seeking their approval. "Is it okay?"

"Yes." Katherine gave him an encouraging smile and a kiss on the cheek. "It's perfect." Flashbulbs popped, catching Katherine and Billy together.

Lynn leaned close to Billy and said very softly, "Why don't you find our table? I'll be along in just a minute." As soon as Billy was out of earshot, Lynn turned her attention to Katherine. "Are you feeling okay? You don't look as though you've been sleeping or eating properly."

Their eyes remained locked for several moments. As if measuring her words, Lynn said, "I know that whatever is bothering you is none of my business, but if you need a friendly shoulder, I'll be glad to let you use mine. You seemed so happy the past few weeks. You were practically glowing...until this week."

Lynn hesitated a moment before she continued. "I...I'm aware that you and Scott have been dating. He didn't mention it to me specifically, but it was easy to see. If there's anything you'd like to talk about, I promise to keep it just between you and me."

Katherine gave Lynn a warm hug. "Thank you. Maybe we could..." Her eyes misted over. Lynn's support meant so much to her. She took a calming breath. "Thank you for your offer. I might take you up on it one of these days." She quickly composed herself and went on with the business of greeting people.

****

Scott stood just inside the door of the ballroom. His throat felt tight and dry. He tried to swallow to lessen the feeling. As soon as he stepped through the door, he spotted Katherine sharing a hug with his mother, then hurrying off. His heart skipped a beat, and his pulse raced. An unbearable emptiness swept through him as his stomach twisted into knots. He should never have gone through with this. Seeing her again only heightened his loneliness and despair...his overwhelming need for her.

She gave off sparkle, shine, and glamour. She was breathtakingly beautiful. Her long beaded gown hugged her curves, the turquoise color an exact match for those incredible eyes he could not get out of his mind. Her smile dazzled everyone she spoke with as she made her way through the growing crowd.

He wanted to leave, but his feet refused to move. His panic grew when her gaze fell on him. As much as he didn't like the reality of it, he couldn't deny that it would require very little effort on her part to have him exactly where she wanted him again. He steeled his determination. He could not allow that to happen.

He wanted to touch her, to hold her, to kiss her, to

consume her in a blaze of passion. He wanted things to be the way he thought they were a week ago, before he discovered the truth. His body stiffened as he braced himself against the overpowering temptation of her nearness. He forced himself to hurry across the room and backstage.

****

Katherine watched Scott walk quickly away. He could not duck her the entire evening. Their relationship was far from being over. She loved him, and she knew he loved her. This stubborn pride of his did more than make her angry. It spurred her resolve. He was not going to get away from her this easily. She had never wanted anyone or anything more than she wanted Scott Blake. No sir, their relationship was far from over.

With the start of the auction only minutes away, Liz talked excitedly with Katherine. "This is the biggest crowd we've ever had. I've even heard rumblings of sizable amounts of money, not already pledged money, but new donations." Liz looked around the ballroom at the glittering array of people. "Well, let's get started."

Liz stepped onstage. The audience immediately quieted. "Good evening, ladies and gentlemen. I'm Liz Torrance. Welcome to our fifth annual charity bachelor auction. If anyone doesn't have a program listing our bachelors and their date packages, please hold up your hand and we'll get one to you." She looked across the crowd. "Okay, it seems we're all set."

Katherine remained at the back of the room. Liz had things well in hand, as usual. All the bachelors would be introduced and seated on the stage. As their turn came, they would step to the podium and give a description of their date package, as briefly outlined in the program, then explain why they had chosen that particular package. She scanned her program. Scott was listed as thirteenth out of fifteen. Number thirteen. Maybe some thought of that as an unlucky number, but not her.

The auction progressed smoothly with everyone in the spirit of the occasion. Two of the bachelors, a football player and a baseball player, elicited some hefty bids.

She had been watching Scott very closely. She was sure no one else could tell, but she saw it in his eyes, in his body language. He would have preferred to be walking barefoot on hot coals through the fires of hell than to be on that stage. A nervous twinge tightened in her stomach. He was up next.

The bidding started immediately and escalated quickly. Four different women were bidding on him. The surprise on his face increased as the price rose higher and higher. Bidding reached the same ten-thousand-dollar level that had won the football player. Liz asked if there were any more bids as she prepared to close the bidding on Scott.

There was a brief moment of silence.

Katherine's voice carried forward from the back of the ballroom. "Fifteen thousand dollars."

A gasp from the audience buzzed loudly through the room, and several flashes from photographers' cameras blinded her. Liz seemed momentarily startled. Stunned more accurately described Scott's visible reaction.

Liz immediately recovered her composure. "Well, is there anyone who cares to top that?" She looked out over the audience. "No? That's it, then. Sold for fifteen thousand dollars."

Following the established procedure, Katherine went up onstage to claim her prize. The audience applauded while cameras recorded everything. She linked her arm with his and maneuvered him offstage to the tables reserved for the bachelors and their dates.

His muscles tensed as she touched his arm, but that didn't stop the tingles of excitement that raced through her body when her hand brushed against his. Butterflies flitted around her stomach. This had to work. It just had to. Somehow, she had to find some time when they could be alone so she could make him listen to her, make him understand. It might mean telling him everything about her childhood and her marriage. She had intended to tell him, but not under these conditions. However, if that was what she had to do to make him understand why her grandfather had initiated the investigation, then that's what she would do.

Scott battled his anger. As soon as they were seated, he whispered through clenched teeth, "Wasn't it enough for you to make a fool out of me in private without extending your little game to make a fool out of me in public, too?"

She kept her voice low, not wanting to attract any more attention than they already were. "You left me no choice. You kept ignoring my invitation to talk this out."

"There's nothing to talk about."

"There's a great deal to talk about, and one way or the other, you're going to listen to what I have to say."

"You don't seriously expect me to go through with this stupid date thing, do you?" His words came out more as an angry statement than a question.

She uttered an emphatic response. "I paid fifteen thousand dollars for the privilege of spending a weekend with you in Yosemite. I expect to get my money's worth."

His jaw tightened. "Of course…your *money's worth.*" The tension in his face lessened, and a hint of despair crept into his voice. "No one asked you to bid on me."

She turned her most dazzling smile on him. "If you recall, you asked me to bid on you just last Sunday."

"Last Sunday was a lifetime ago." His mumbled response was tinged with sadness as he looked away from her. "A weak moment of foolishness."

The closing of the auction portion of the evening's festivities interrupted their strained and adversarial conversation. There was no opportunity for Katherine to have even a few minutes alone with Scott, no chance to explain to him. People were everywhere, they were constantly surrounded. Liz spoke to all the bachelors and their dates, making sure they would all be at the party. There would be press coverage, more publicity photos.

****

Scott had hoped to slip quietly away without any further involvement, but circumstances dictated that it wasn't going to happen that way. He would be the object of even more attention and speculation if he didn't show up at the party. He retrieved his car from the hotel parking and reluctantly drove to the party location, trepidation and a sinking feeling of dread filling his consciousness.

He pulled his car over to the side of the road a

block away from RJ Fairchild's house. He needed a quiet moment to think and collect himself before entering the glare of the party. He had pretty much been the center of attention following the auction, almost an object of curiosity because of Katherine's bid. Knowing his every move and every word were being closely observed left him extremely uncomfortable.

A sigh of resignation escaped his lips. He just wanted it to be done. He put the car in gear and continued down the street.

Scott turned his car over to the parking attendant and started up the walkway. He paused for a moment as he looked around. The Fairchild mansion buzzed with activity. The place reeked of big-time, old-line money. Every light in the house had been turned on. Definitely one of the gala social events of the year.

A nervousness jittered through his stomach as a chill ran up his spine. He did not want to be there. He took a calming breath and walked up the steps to the front door. The attendant took his invitation, and he stepped into the frenzy of activity.

Katherine was at his side immediately. She seemed to have appeared from out of nowhere. She grabbed his hand, tugging insistently. "Come with me. We're going to talk."

He removed his hand from her grasp, refusing to follow. "How many times do I need to tell you we have nothing to talk about? I won't be a pawn in whatever this game is, Ms. Fairchild."

"Scott, please… There is no game. There never was." Her voice conveyed an anguish that made him want to give her what she wanted. "That file is not what you think. I can explain it if you'll just listen. Let's go to a quiet room and—"

"Don't do this to me, Katherine." He couldn't keep the aching emptiness out of his voice. "Let me heal my wounds so I can get on with my life."

"*Your* wounds!" Her anger exploded. "What about my wounds?"

His anger flared to match hers. "Why would you have any wounds, Ms. Fairchild?" He glanced around as if to make sure no one had heard them, then lowered his voice. "It was your game. You won every round. You had me all the way. You're the winner." He lowered his voice. "Now, let me go. I don't like this game. I don't want to play anymore."

Determination took hold of Katherine. "We have plenty to talk about, and you're going to listen to me even if I have to tie you to a chair and—"

"There you are, Katherine." Jim Dalton's voice drew her attention as he approached. "I've a couple of people here you should really meet." He turned a questioning look toward Scott. "You don't mind if I steal her away for a few minutes, do you? I promise she'll be right back."

Scott offered a pleasant smile. "No, I don't mind."

Chapter Ten

"Are you all right, dear?" Scott's mother placed her hand on his arm. "That's a very strange expression on your face. It would seem to me that any man who just had five women fighting over him to the ultimate tune of fifteen thousand dollars should look happier than you do."

He opened his eyes and quickly collected himself. "Mom, uh..." For the first time he noticed Billy. He was grateful for anything that would allow him to change the conversation. "Billy—a suit and tie?"

"Jeez, why does everyone keep making a big deal out of it?" Billy, obviously embarrassed, put forth an effort to regain control of the situation as he glared at Scott. "What d'ya think? I'm plannin' on diggin' ditches the rest of my life?"

"Oh? What are your plans?" Scott tried to suppress his amusement at Billy's attempt at being tough in unfamiliar circumstances.

"You can tell John Barclay to look out. I'm after his job. And then"—he leveled a challenging look at Scott—"I think I might like your job. Sittin' in a big office and pushing paper around a desk just might be to my liking."

"Lynn, don't you look lovely this evening!" Jim Dalton had returned, having left Katherine to discuss charity business with some prospective contributors.

"There's dancing in the other room. Would you honor me?" He extended his arm to her as he offered a smile that held more than mere courtesy for an acquaintance.

"It's been quite a while since I last danced, but if you promise not to complain if I step on your toes, I would be delighted." She linked her arm with his, and they disappeared through the crowd.

Scott watched them with more than idle curiosity. It had been five years since his father's death. His mother was a vibrant, youthful woman. She should be dating, enjoying a social life that consisted of more than her lady friends. Jim Dalton seemed to be a very nice man, a widower himself. Scott approved.

"Looks like, your ol'—I mean, looks like Lynn's got a boyfriend." Billy grinned mischievously.

Scott cocked his head and gave Billy an appraising look. "You don't miss much, do you?"

"I see everything, man." Billy looked across the room at Katherine, still busily involved in her conversation, then back at Scott. "I see *everything*."

Scott shifted his weight uncomfortably.

"You know, Jenny keeps askin' for you. She doesn't understand why you aren't there." Having made that pointed comment, Billy abruptly turned and wandered off toward the buffet, leaving Scott standing all alone.

Billy's comment about Jenny bothered him. He had missed seeing the little girl, missed her giggle and the way her blonde curls bounced up and down, missed the family times they had shared—Katherine, Jenny, and him. He was not, however, allowed the solitude of his thoughts for long. A moment later he was swept up in a whirlwind of activity.

Two hours had passed when he saw his mother, Jim Dalton, and RJ Fairchild headed his way. A knot tightened in Scott's stomach. He had been able to avoid RJ for the entire evening. He had started to believe that he might be home free.

His mother introduced them. The firmness of the old man's handshake and the strength he possessed surprised Scott. RJ Fairchild had to be in his early to mid-eighties and had been confined to a wheelchair due to failing health. However, the man whose hand he had just shaken demonstrated none of those characteristics.

"So you're the young man who has created such a stir. It seems to be all I hear anymore—Scott this, Scott that. Even little Jenny chatters on and on about you. You seem to be everyone's topic of conversation, especially Katherine's." RJ paused a moment as if to collect his thoughts, then proceeded. "I'm probably a little too protective of Katherine—"

"Grandfather!" Katherine's voice abruptly cut off his words. She looked about nervously, her gaze flitting from Jim to Scott's mother to Scott and finally coming to rest on her grandfather. "You weren't about to divulge any family secrets, were you?"

Her poorly concealed attempt to hide her nervousness, a nervousness almost bordering on anxiety, grabbed Scott's attention. It was very out of character for her. He caught the quick look that passed between her and her grandfather. There was definitely more going on than was immediately apparent.

She quickly changed the subject. Spotting Billy across the room, she called him over. "Billy, I'd like you to meet someone. Grandfather, this is Billy Sanchez. You've heard me speak of him."

Billy struck a tough stance as RJ looked him over, then extended his hand. "Hello, young man. It's nice to meet you." Billy shook hands with him. A camera flashed, catching Billy and RJ Fairchild together. "Katherine has mentioned you on several occasions."

Billy shifted uncomfortably from one foot to the other.

Scott's mother quickly reached out and put her hand on his shoulder to calm his nervousness. "I think now might be a good time for your announcement." She gave him an encouraging smile.

"Yeah, well…if you want to tell them, I guess it's okay with me." Billy was obviously embarrassed, just short of blushing.

Lynn turned her attention to include everyone present in their little group. "Ladies and gentlemen, I have an announcement I'd like to make. As of last Thursday evening, Mr. Billy Sanchez has passed all the necessary high school equivalency tests for his general education diploma. He's a full-fledged high school graduate."

Billy looked at the floor and mumbled his response. "It's not that big a deal."

Katherine gave him a big hug and a kiss on the cheek, her enthusiasm clearly evident. "That's marvelous. I'm so proud of you, Billy."

Jim and RJ both congratulated him. Scott put his arm around Billy's shoulders and gave him a big smile. "So that's what has been going on with you and Mom. It seems you were very serious when you said you wanted my job. You're off to a good start."

Scott turned toward his mother. "You may be able to take the woman out of the classroom, but you can't take the teacher out of the woman." He gave her a quick wink. "Now tell me, doesn't this beat working in your garden?"

The hour grew late, the party finally winding to a close. The majority of the guests had gone home. Scott had been trying to leave from the moment fate intervened to interrupt Katherine's attempts to get him alone. He glanced at his watch. "It's getting late." He directed his comments toward RJ while extending a gracious smile. "I'm sure you must be tired of all these intruders by now and would like your house back."

"Not at all, young man. I look forward to this gathering every year. I particularly enjoy the time after most of the guests have departed. It gives me an opportunity to have some good conversation with interesting people." RJ headed his wheelchair toward the garden room as he continued to talk, forcing Scott to follow him. "Now, tell me…"

The next couple of hours passed quickly for Scott. Much to his surprise, he found RJ easy to talk with and very interesting. Not at all the intimidating figure he had anticipated.

The realization of how quiet the house had become gradually penetrated Scott's reality. The sounds of a party had disappeared. He glanced at his watch, surprised to find that it was after three o'clock in the morning. "I had no idea it was so late. I must apologize for overstaying my welcome." He got to his feet and extended his hand toward RJ. "It's been a real pleasure meeting you."

"The pleasure's been all mine, Scott. I hope I'll be seeing more of you in the future."

He didn't know exactly how to respond to RJ's

statement. It seemed to have been made more emphatically than a mere courtesy reply. Panic welled inside him as he realized the full impact of the statement, RJ's subtle probing for information. Just how much did he know? How much had Katherine told him? He needed to get away.

It suddenly occurred to him that Katherine might be the only one left in the house, all the guests having gone home. Panic overtook him again. He might not be able to avoid being alone with her. "I…uh…really need to be going. I have a long drive back to Tiburon. It's been a pleasure meeting you. Good night, RJ."

"Good night, Scott."

He hurried from the garden room, hoping to make it to the front door. He did not see anyone as he made his way through the house. He had almost reached the front door when he spotted Katherine sitting in a chair in the foyer. She did not see him. Her eyes were closed, and she appeared to be asleep. He paused a moment to watch her. She seemed so very alone, a little girl lost in a big house. He wanted to go to her, put his arms around her, to hold her…to take care of her.

She had been very persistent about wanting to talk to him. Was the fifteen-thousand-dollar bid a desperate attempt to force a discussion or merely her way of showing him, and everyone else, that he was no more than just another of her many possessions, bought and paid for? As he looked at her now—her shoes on the floor, her legs curled up under her, her head resting on the chair wing—all he could think about was how much he loved her.

Scott didn't know what to think anymore. Reluctantly, he turned and walked out the front door.

****

Katherine's phone kept ringing all day Sunday, one call after another, starting at eight o'clock that morning before she was even awake. The Sunday newspaper carried a full array of pictures and stories about the auction and fundraising party. Everyone was very excited.

Liz was the first to call. She had been up all night and had just finished tallying the total dollar figure of money raised. Even though thoroughly exhausted, her enthusiasm communicated itself to Katherine. "It's the biggest one to date and pledges are still coming in. The office phone started ringing an hour ago even though it's Sunday and the offices are supposed to be closed."

"No kidding?" Katherine scooted up against the headboard to sit cross-legged on her bed and listen to Liz read off some of the major contributions. "Wow, one hundred thousand dollars from Richard Bentley. Grandpa must have really twisted his arm. I think that old tightwad still has the first dollar he ever earned."

"Here's one I think you'll really like. It's a check in the amount of fifty dollars drawn on a brand-new checking account—from one Billy Sanchez."

Katherine's eyes misted over. Not only had Billy finished high school, worked hard at his job, bought a suit and tie, and even opened a bank account, he had actually made a donation to the charity. She was so proud of him.

"You should have seen him, Kat. He was so embarrassed he didn't know what to do. Just before he left RJ's house, he came over to me, stammered nervously, then shoved the check into my hand and beat it out the door as fast as he could. He was so cute. I called the center this morning to thank him. Cheryl was there. She said he was sound asleep, so I told her not to wake him."

As soon as she finished talking to Liz, Katherine went to the front door and picked up her newspaper from the porch. A frown creased her brow as she scanned the society section. She was in almost every one of the photos. Once again, the Fairchild name had dominated the newspaper more than the name of the charity or the reason for the event. There was even a picture of her kissing Billy's cheek and one of Billy shaking hands with RJ. She chuckled to herself as she wondered how Billy would explain that to the guys on the construction crew, assuming his co-workers actually looked at the society pages.

The rest of the day went pretty much the same way as the morning, one phone call after another. But no call from Scott.

****

Scott's day gave him far too much time to dwell on his misery. Even though it was early afternoon, he sat on his couch drinking his morning coffee and reading the Sunday paper. It had been after four in the morning when he arrived home and after sunrise before he had finally gotten to sleep. He had been unable to turn off his thoughts of Katherine and how much he wanted her. Not only did she occupy his conscious thoughts, but she also dominated his dreams as well.

As he scanned the articles about the auction and the fund-raising party, a new reality hit him. Almost every photo was of Katherine doing something or talking to someone. She was mentioned all the way through every article. But that was not the way it had been—not at all.

Katherine had stayed in the background during the entire auction, except for her one and only bid, and had let Liz take charge. It was the same way at the party afterward. She had maintained a low profile and directed the majority of attention to the others who were present.

He put down his paper. Was this typical of the way it had been all along? Katherine trying to stay out of the center of publicity, but her name making it impossible for her? That was certainly the way he had perceived it last night. The newspaper account did not give an accurate portrayal at all. He reflected on her moment of sad resignation when he had asked her how she put up with always being in the public eye, and her only response had been that one eventually got used to it. Perhaps the fifteen-thousand-dollar bid really was...

He felt a glimmer of hope start to break through his despair.

What was left of the afternoon passed quickly. Scott grabbed his car keys and left his house. He pulled his car into the circular drive at his mother's house and hurried up to the front door. He probably should have called first to make sure she was home, but instead, he had impulsively driven there.

It had been quite a while since they had shared Sunday evening dinner at the little Sausalito restaurant that had been a family favorite when he was growing up. His mind was too full of thoughts of Katherine and Jenny, of how he missed the times they had shared. He desperately wanted, actually *needed*, to recapture that feeling of family closeness.

"I'm afraid I'm not quite ready..." His mother's eyes widened when she opened the door. "Scott, dear.

What are you doing here?"

He offered her a teasing grin. "Is that any way to greet your favorite son?" The grin faded as he noticed the way she was dressed. She had not been lounging around the house. She was dressed to go out. "Am I interrupting something? Those aren't exactly your working in the garden clothes."

"Of course you're not interrupting. Don't stand out there on the porch. Come in."

He closed the door after entering the house. "I thought we might go to Sausalito for Sunday night dinner if you're not busy. We haven't done that for quite a while."

"Well, actually...I already have a dinner engagement for this evening."

He lifted his eyebrows as he cocked his head. "Really? With whom?" Suddenly, the realization hit him. He let a knowing grin spread across his face. "You have a date with Jim Dalton."

A blush covered her cheeks as she lowered her eyelids. "It's not really a *date*. Dating is for young people, like you and Katherine. We're simply having dinner together, that's all."

The mention of Katherine chilled his good humor.

"What's wrong, dear? You've seemed quite out of sorts lately. Are you and Katherine having problems?"

He tried to cover his inner turmoil. "There's nothing wrong..."

She leveled a stern look at him. "You know I try never to interfere in your personal life. There's nothing worse than a grown man who has a mother always meddling in his life as though he were still a little boy."

"However..." His voice held a full measure of

169

caution.

"However, I have something to say, and I want you to listen." She sat on the couch and motioned for him to join her. "You know I loved your father very much. He was the kindest, most caring man I ever knew. He was also the most stubborn. Well, my favorite son, I believe you've surpassed him in the stubborn department."

Scott looked at her, shocked by her words. "What are you talking about?"

"I'm talking about you and Katherine. The poor girl is obviously distraught, and you're a mess. I don't know what's going on or what has happened, but I'm sure your stubborn attitude is contributing to the problem, acerbating the situation rather than helping." She gave him a loving pat on the cheek, then stood up. "That's all I'm going to say on the subject. Now, I have an engage…" She gave him an impish grin. "I have a *date,* and I'm not quite ready yet, so I'll have to ask you to run along."

Without further ado, she ushered Scott out her front door just as Jim Dalton pulled into the driveway.

Instead of going home, Scott drove to his neighborhood waterfront pub just a couple of blocks from his house.

"Give me a beer, Terry." Scott slid onto the end barstool. He grabbed a small packet of peanuts from a large bowl, ripped it open, and tossed a couple of them in his mouth as he stared out the window at the ocean.

The bartender poured a draft beer and set it in front of him. "Here you go." He waved his hand in front of Scott's face. "Hey, Earth to Scott, Earth to Scott…"

"Huh? Oh, sorry, Terry. I've got a lot on my mind."

"Hi, Scott." The sultry voice of Susan, the cocktail waitress, drifted over him as she slipped her arm around his shoulders. "It's been a while since we've seen you. Where have you been keeping yourself?"

He ignored her obvious attempts to flirt with him. "I've been busy lately, a new construction project…a shopping center in San Rafael."

Terry laughed an open, outgoing laugh. "That's not all you've been busy with, if this morning's paper can be believed. That was quite some picture of you and the famous Katherine Fairchild."

He frowned. "It was only a charity thing, that's all."

"Tell me, Scott…" Susan brushed her body against his, being anything but subtle. "Exactly what makes you worth fifteen thousand dollars?"

He stared at her without really seeing her. A horde of thoughts rampaged through his mind. What made him worth fifteen thousand dollars? Certainly not proving a point or playing a game. He reached into his pocket and put some money on the bar.

"Here's for the beer." He rose from the barstool and headed for the door. "See ya later."

He drove straight home and immediately walked out onto his deck. The brisk evening air soothed his confusion. His mother's words played through his mind, and the image of Katherine curled up in the chair by the front door of RJ's house kept popping into his consciousness. His overwhelming love for her filled him. He thought he had everything figured out, but now he didn't seem to be able to separate reality from hurt pride.

****

The nonstop phone calls finally came to an end, and Katherine breathed a sigh of relief, glad to have an opportunity to sit back and relax. She felt drained, both physically and emotionally. The auction had worn her out, but the added strain of her emotional turmoil had left her exhausted. Several times during the day, she had reached for the phone to call Scott. Sometimes, an incoming call made that impossible. At other times, she paused, then withdrew her hand from the phone.

She had been most unhappy with herself for falling asleep in the chair by the door. When her grandfather woke her and told her Scott had already left, despair had settled over her. It had been her last chance to get him alone. She knew RJ had done his best to keep Scott occupied until all the guests had departed, but she had blown it. She had been too exhausted to keep her eyes open one minute longer.

She shivered, and a sob caught in her throat. She had gotten very little sleep last night and hadn't even bothered to get dressed after she woke up. Now it was time to go to bed again. Perhaps tomorrow would be a better day.

She lay in bed staring at the ceiling, wondering what the future would bring, wondering if she could go on without Scott.

Katherine Sutton Fairchild, listen to yourself. You sound like a quitter. A new surge of determination hit her. *Fate isn't something that just happens from out of nowhere. You make your life choices and create your opportunities. I may have missed this opportunity, but I'll see to it that there's another one. This is not over, and it won't be over until Scott has his arms wrapped around me and is saying how much he loves me. One way or the other, that's the way it's going to be.*

Katherine pounded her pillow into a comfortable shape, turned over, and closed her eyes.

****

Scott had retired early after being up so late last night. He lay in bed staring at the ceiling, his mind trying to put some organization to his confused thoughts. The past week had been the most miserable of his life. That much he knew for sure. He finally fell into a restless sleep, bits and pieces of dreams running through his subconscious, snatches of information trying to connect into some sort of reality.

Scott awoke with a start. It was already daylight. The sheets and covers were a tangled mess attesting to his restless night of tossing and turning. He did have one very clear, crystallized thought in his head. He had been wrong to ignore Katherine's attempts to talk to him, to refuse to listen to her. His mother had been right. He was a stubborn, damn fool. Maybe those had not been her exact words, but that was precisely what she meant.

He took a quick shower, dressed, and went to the phone. With a slightly trembling hand, he dialed Katherine's number. The phone rang several times, but no one answered, not even her voice mail. He finally hung up.

****

As Katherine rinsed the shampoo from her hair with her head under the shower spray, she thought she heard the phone ringing. She turned off the water and listened but heard nothing. She quickly finished, dried her hair, dressed, and dashed out the door to her breakfast meeting. After the meeting, she stopped by the florist and picked out a flower arrangement. She paused as she thought about the message for the accompanying card.

The next item on her agenda? Shopping. It was Halloween, and she would be taking Jenny trick or treating that evening. She had been looking forward to sharing Jenny's first costume and first trick or treat. She smiled as she visualized the little girl's excitement earlier, how her face had glowed as she talked about being a fairy princess with a crown and a magic wand. There was only one thing missing that kept everything from being perfect—Scott.

The warm glow faded. Jenny had wanted Scott to go with them, and Katherine had not known what to tell her, so she said that he was very busy with work and she did not think he would be able to go. Her heart filled with sorrow when she'd seen the look of disappointment on Jenny's face.

****

Scott drove directly to the construction site in San Rafael before going to the office. He had a progress meeting with John Barclay in the office trailer, then took a look around the site. Everything looked good with the project right on schedule in spite of the inventory audit interruption.

The crew was on a morning coffee break. He noticed a group of men gathered around Billy, one of them holding Sunday's newspaper. As he passed them, he heard Billy saying, "Yeah, me and Kat go back a long way." He caught a moment's eye contact with Billy, pausing long enough to give him a quick nod of approval.

Billy clearly enjoyed his new celebrity status.

As soon as Scott arrived at his office, he tried calling Katherine again. Still no answer. Had she forgotten to turn on her answering machine or was she purposely avoiding him the way he had avoided her? He tried her cell phone, but it was turned off. He called two more times that morning, then tried her at the charity's offices. They had not seen her. He called the Oakland center. He heard the cool reserve in Cheryl's voice when she told him Katherine was not there.

Shortly after lunch, Amelia walked into his office carrying an arrangement of flowers, her irritation clearly evident. "Mr. Blake, this is the last straw. Please do something about this." She handed him the sealed envelope containing the card that accompanied the flowers.

"I think those flowers would look nice in your office." He smiled as he took the envelope from her.

This new attitude on his part obviously caught Amelia off guard. She hesitated for a moment, her brow wrinkling into a slight frown, then turned and carried the flowers to her office. She tactfully closed the office door behind her.

Scott's heart pounded. With trembling fingers, he removed the card from the envelope. *I'm taking Jenny trick or treating this evening. Please come.*

He held the card in his hand and read it a second time. A warm feeling of happiness settled inside him, the first calm moment he had felt since that terrible Sunday night a week ago.

He glanced at his watch. He needed to find a Halloween   costume.

Chapter Eleven

Katherine swung by the Oakland center to pick up Jenny. She did not see Cheryl and did not have time to wait for her to return. She wanted to get home before the evening rush hour traffic piled up on the freeway and clogged the Bay Bridge.

Her grandfather had promised to come to her house to have an early dinner with them. He had even agreed to stay the evening and hand out candy to the children who came to the door while she was out with Jenny. She chuckled. What would the board members of the numerous Fairchild enterprises say if they knew the powerful RJ Fairchild personally handed out trick or treat candy?

Her grandfather had taken her trick or treating every Halloween from the time she was a little girl, even before her mother had…

Katherine glanced toward Jenny, strapped securely into the car seat. *I promise you. I'll see to it that you're never denied the joys and pleasures due all children as they grow up, that you'll always have someone who loves you.*

She reached out and touched the little girl's blonde curls.

Jenny turned toward Katherine. "Will Scott be there?" Her big brown eyes held innocence and questions.

"I don't know, precious. He…he said he'd try." Disappointment filtered over the child's face. Katherine quickly turned her attention back to the road.

As soon as they arrived at her house, she took Jenny up to her bedroom to get her dressed for her big trick or treat adventure.

Jenny's excitement wouldn't let her stand still. She kept jumping up and down and clapping her hands as Katherine tried to get her into her costume. Dinner had already been prepared and only needed to be heated when RJ arrived. Jenny and Katherine both heard the car as it pulled up into the driveway. The little girl ran from Katherine's bedroom and down the stairs. "Scott…Scott."

"Jenny, wait a minute. Don't go so fast, you'll hurt yourself." Katherine went after her, surprised at how quickly the child had slipped out of her reach.

****

Scott felt as if he had been in and out of every costume shop in San Francisco only to find the same answer—sold out of anything and everything even remotely close to his size. Finally he settled on just a mask. The afternoon had slipped toward evening. He wanted to make sure he made it to Katherine's house before they left on their trick or treat rounds. He had tried several times, unsuccessfully, to reach her by phone to tell her he would be there.

He pulled up to Katherine's house and parked at the curb. A shiver of panic cut through him when he saw the limo in the driveway and the police car at the curb. He quickly went to the door and rang the bell, then impatiently knocked.

"RJ!" Even though he instinctively knew the limo

belonged to Katherine's grandfather, Scott was still surprised to see him opening the front door. Then a deep fear spread through him as he saw the two police officers standing on the other side of the living room, engaged in very serious conversation. One of the officers left, excusing himself as he brushed by Scott and out the front door.

Knots of apprehension twisted in the pit of his stomach as he entered the house. In a voice barely above a whisper, he managed to force out some words. "What's going on? Katherine...is she..."

"Katherine is fine. She's in her bedroom."

Scott immediately turned toward the stairs, but RJ stopped him.

"One moment, young man." RJ propelled his wheelchair to where Scott stood at the foot of the staircase.

"Katherine is fine physically. Emotionally, it's a different story. Jenny is missing." A sharp jolt of anxiety swept through Scott as he listened to RJ. "She heard a car pull up in front of the house and thought it was you. She got away from Katherine and was out the door before Katherine could stop her. She simply disappeared into the darkness. Katherine spent half an hour looking for her, then called the police."

"Why would Jenny have thought it was me?" As soon as the words were out of his mouth, he realized how stupid they sounded. He didn't even know why he had said them.

"Because she has been asking for you all week, kept asking Katherine if you were going trick or treating with them." RJ leveled a cool look at Scott as if he could read the thoughts and feelings swirling around inside him. "Katherine didn't know what to say. She didn't want to tell the little girl yes, then have her be disappointed and hurt when you didn't show up."

The pain stabbed deep inside Scott. His own misery of the past week had blocked out any and all consideration of what anyone else was going through. He had selfishly wallowed in self-pity without a hint of consideration for anyone else. Again, he turned toward the stairs. "I have to go to Katherine. She must be terribly upset about Jenny... And I'm sure she's very angry with me."

"Before you go up there..." RJ reached out and actually grabbed Scott's arm to halt him. "I want to tell you a story. A story about a little girl."

A hint of irritation crept through Scott. He didn't have time for this. He wanted to get to Katherine, comfort her, and ask her forgiveness, beg for it if that was what it took. He touched the small velvet box in his jacket pocket. He wanted to tell her how much he loved her. "I know all about Jenny's background."

"I'm not talking about Jenny." He gave Scott a stern look. "I want to tell you a story about a little girl who everyone thought had everything a little girl could possibly want. Now, mind you, this is just a story. You can put whatever interpretation on it you want."

****

Katherine stood on the deck off her bedroom staring out into the darkness, her arms crossed as she hugged her shoulders against the cold, damp ocean air. She felt numb inside. Tears trickled down her cheeks. How could she have been so careless as to let Jenny slip out the door like that? *If anything happens to her, I'll never be able to forgive myself.*

"Katherine?"

The soft voice startled her. She had not been aware of anyone entering the room. She slowly turned around until she faced Scott. At first, she didn't know what to do, so she just stood there, her fears covering her like a blanket. Finally, she spoke, her voice quavering with emotion. "She's all alone out there, so lost and alone."

"Kind of like you?"

She stared at him, not comprehending what he said. Then the light of realization hit her, and her gaze immediately dropped to the floor.

He walked to her side, placed his fingertips under her chin, and raised her face until he could look into her eyes. "I've behaved like a first-rate jackass and a damn fool."

Katherine didn't know what she felt. Her despair over Jenny had left her traumatized, yet the sight of Scott and the sound of his voice warmed her, easing that despair. She let herself be folded in the security of his arms. She didn't have the energy to engage in any verbal jousting. She was just thankful he was there. She said the first thing that came to her mind. "That's absolutely correct. You've been behaving like a real jackass." Her words were true and said without any hint of anger or recrimination.

He smiled. "I see we've found an area of agreement. Now, let me try for another one." He took in a steadying breath. "Can you ever forgive me?"

She shuddered as an intense wave of emotion washed over her. She tried her best to hold back the sobs. "He told you, didn't he? He promised me he wouldn't. I wanted you to come back because you wanted to, not because you felt sorry for me—poor little rich girl and all that."

"All he told me was a story, only a story." Scott pulled her closer to him, holding her tighter as he caressed her back and twined his fingers in her hair. She rested her head against his shoulder. His heart beat faster under her cheek. "Please forgive me, Katherine. More than anything I want to erase this past week. It's been the most horrible week of my life. That file doesn't matter. What does matter is that we're together."

He lowered his head and lightly brushed his lips against hers. He cradled her head to his shoulder as he rested his cheek against her hair. "I know this isn't the perfect time, but I love you, Katherine. I love you very much. I don't want us ever to be apart again."

Euphoria shot through her unlike anything she had ever experienced. She sent up a silent prayer. *Please let it be true.* "Oh, Scott. I can't even describe how much I love you. I've loved you from the first moment we shook hands in your office. I know that sounds absurd like something out of one of those romance novels, but it's true."

The muscles in his shoulders relaxed. "Then you're a little quicker than I am. I don't think I fell in love with you until a couple of hours later, in the elevator at the Hyatt." He continued to hold her, stroke her hair, and caress her shoulders.

The shared moment when they confessed their love for each other had been unusually subdued, given the nature of their words. They were torn between two extremes—the overwhelming joy of their shared love and the very real anxiety over the missing Jenny. What should have been a moment of unbridled celebration remained tinged with an increasing sense of anxiety as the hour grew later and later.

Katherine and Scott sat on the couch in her bedroom, his arm protectively around her shoulders as he held her to him. The doorbell had been ringing all evening. Each time she heard it she jumped to her feet, but it was always the same. Only children trick or treating. RJ stayed downstairs and took care of the candy chores, shooing Katherine and Scott back upstairs.

She raised her head from Scott's shoulder and looked into his eyes. "It's been over two hours. Where could she be?"

He brushed his lips gently against hers. "I'm sure she's okay. Try not to worry." A frown wrinkled his brow. He obviously didn't feel anywhere near as positive as the words he used.

She emitted a sigh of despair as the doorbell rang again.

"I don't know what I'll do if anything happens to her." A shudder moved through her. She tried to suppress the sobs as the tears welled in her eyes. She clung to him, needing and taking the strength and comfort he provided.

Katherine had leaned against Scott and closed her eyes just for a moment when Scott suddenly moved her upright. "Katherine...look."

A sound had caught his attention, and next to the stairs, a sliding door opened. RJ emerged from the small elevator. Sitting in his lap was an adorable little girl dressed as a fairy princess. Jenny giggled as RJ pushed the lever to guide the wheelchair into the room.

"Jenny!" Katherine jumped up from the couch and

ran across the room. She snatched the little girl away from RJ and wrapped her arms around the giggling child. She hugged Jenny tightly against her body, tears of relief and happiness streaming down her cheeks.

"Are you all right, my little precious?"

She turned toward RJ. "Where did they find her?"

"According to the police officer who brought her back, she joined a group of children who were trick or treating and went from house to house with them. The mother who was accompanying the kids didn't realize she had an extra one until an hour later. She tried to find out who Jenny was and where she lived, but the only thing she could learn was that the little girl had been *at Kat's house,* which made no sense to her, so she called the police."

"She seems to be okay."

"She's just fine. The policeman said she was having a grand time."

Katherine felt Scott's arm slip around her shoulders, felt the warmth of his touch. She covered his hand with hers, relishing the sensation of his closeness.

"Scott…Scott." Jenny wiggled in Katherine's arms as she tried to reach him, her blonde curls bouncing up and down with her excitement. "We went to a house that had a witch. Everybody was scared 'cept me. Another house had a ghost, but it wasn't really a ghost. It was just a man dressed up like a ghost."

Scott took the giggling little girl from Katherine's arms. Jenny's tiny hand patted him on the cheek, then she wrapped her arms around his neck.

"Well…" RJ nodded, indicating his pleasure at the turn of events. "It looks like you don't need me here. I'll go back downstairs and tend to my candy duties."

With that, he propelled his wheelchair toward the elevator.

"Jenny, precious, I was so worried about you. You shouldn't run off like that. You could have been hurt. Scott came to go trick or treating with us. He's been very worried about you, too."

"That's right, Jenny." Scott touched the little girl's cheek in a loving gesture. "We've all been very worried."

Jenny yawned as she snuggled in Scott's arms. She had been involved in a very big adventure for a three-year-old and was exhausted. Scott carried her downstairs to the guest room. Katherine folded back the covers, then he laid Jenny in the bed. Katherine removed Jenny's shoes. The little girl had fallen asleep still wearing her costume.

Katherine covered her with the blanket and kissed her on the cheek. "Good night, Jenny."

Katherine and Scott watched as Jenny slept peacefully in the big bed, seemingly without a care in the world. They were each lost in their own thoughts. He turned out the light, and they went back upstairs. Relief settled over each of them, relief that Jenny had been found unharmed. And not only unharmed, apparently delighted with her adventure.

They sat on the couch. Scott drew Katherine to him, his arms holding her in a warm embrace. He ran his fingertips across her cheek as he spoke in a soft, loving voice. "She didn't seem to be upset or frightened. I think she's just fine."

"I hope so." Katherine stifled a yawn. With the crisis resolved, she could give in to her exhaustion.

He kissed her on the cheek. "You're tired. Perhaps

I should go home for now. We can have dinner together tomorrow night."

She looked searchingly into his eyes. "How do I know you'll come back?"

"Katherine…please, Katherine." His arms tightened around her, and his voice turned raspy with emotion. "Please forgive me. I love you so very much." He lowered his head and brushed his lips softly against hers before capturing her mouth in a loving kiss.

Her fingers trembled slightly as she touched them to his cheek. She felt the heat of his passion. A soft kiss with a very deep meaning. "No, don't go. Grandpa will be leaving in a little while. We can be alone, have time to get to know each other again."

"I'd like that…very much," he said, his voice a verbal caress.

"Let's go to the den. You can build a nice fire in the fireplace, and I'll see how the candy supply is holding out. I would imagine most of the trick or treaters have already made the rounds."

Scott paused at the door of the guest room to check on Jenny as Katherine continued on down the stairs. She went to the front door where her grandfather had stationed himself. "Grandpa, how are you doing?"

"I was just about to come and get you. Things are pretty quiet now. I think I can close up shop and have James drive me home." He glanced toward the stairs, as if making sure he and Katherine were alone. He leaned toward her and spoke in a quiet voice. "How are things with you and Scott? It's the way you wanted it to be, isn't it? He did come here on his own."

She tried to give him a stern look but was not able to hold it. "I don't know what to do with you. You

185

promised me you wouldn't interfere, then you turned around and told him about..." Scott may have come to her house on his own, but was he staying because he really loved her or...

"Katherine, I know you sometimes think I'm a meddling old fool, but you know how much I love you. I only want your happiness. You deserve it."

"I know, Grandpa. I know." She leaned over and kissed him on the cheek, then brought him his coat. The chauffeur helped him to his limo. She closed and locked the front door, turned out the porch light, then hurried back to the den.

****

Scott was seated on the floor among the large pillows. He had poured each of them a glass of wine. When he heard Katherine coming up the stairs, he reached to where his jacket rested on the arm of the love seat. He touched the pocket, reassuring himself that the small velvet box was still there. Nervous energy jittered through his veins. She had never said she forgave him. She had told him she loved him, and she had asked him to stay. But she had not told him she forgave his terrible behavior of the last week. He needed to hear those words of forgiveness, to know in his mind that it was so.

Katherine stepped through the den door. The light from the flames lit the room, casting soft shadows on the walls and flickering highlights over her beautiful features. She had a worried, pensive look on her face as she stared into the flames. He loved her so much. He hoped they would be able to put the week behind them and get on with their lives, what he hoped would be their life together.

"I see you've poured the wine. A little trick or treat goody for the adults?" She flashed a dazzling smile.

"No tricks, only a treat," he teased with a responding smile. "Come here and sit down. You look lonely over there all by yourself."

She quickly moved to sit beside him on the large floor pillows. He handed her a glass of wine, allowing his fingers to touch the soft warmth of her hand. He held up his glass, then clinked it against hers. "To you." He looked intently and lovingly into the depths of her eyes. "I love you, Katherine. I love you very much."

The last word choked in his throat, the emotion almost too much for him. "I'm sorry for everything I've put you through. I don't deserve your forgiveness, but please tell me you forgive me anyway. I have to hear you say the words. I have to know it's true."

She looked at him for a long moment, then slowly leaned forward and brushed her lips softly against his. "I love you. Of course I forgive you—this time," she teased. "But don't ever do that to me again." Her manner turned serious. "I don't think I could live through it a second time."

He set his wine glass on the fireplace hearth, enfolded her in his arms, and reveled in her closeness. "What do you want?" He murmured the words in her ear. "What do you want the future to be? What can I do that will make you happy?"

A tremor darted through her body. What was he asking? What was really on his mind? What she wanted more than anything was a home with Scott and Jenny. She wanted them to be a real family. Was she wanting too much?

"I…I don't know." She gazed questioningly into

his eyes, as if searching for answers. "What are you willing to give? How much of a commitment are you ready to make?"

How much of a commitment? An easy question. He had purchased his proof of commitment before they had gone away for the weekend. Now was the time to share it with her. "I think I have an answer to your question right here in my jacket pocket." He withdrew the box.

Katherine's eyes grew wide as she looked at the small velvet box. He opened it, and the diamonds captured and reflected the light from the flames as the ring sparkled against the black velvet background. He took it from the box. With trembling hands, he slipped the exquisite ring on her finger. "Marry me, Katherine. I want to spend the rest of my life with you."

Tears welled in her eyes as she looked at the ring on her finger. "Are you really sure? Do you really want to marry me?"

"Do I want to marry you?" He cupped her face in his hands, kissed her lovingly and deeply. Every bit of love he felt for her coursed through his body. "More than anything in the world I want to marry you."

"It doesn't matter that everywhere I go someone from the press takes my picture? It doesn't matter that I seem always to be in the glare of the public eye even though I don't seek it out and don't want it?"

Scott felt her tremble in his arms and saw the concern in her eyes. "I've already asked myself those same questions, more than once."

"And?"

"And nothing matters other than our being together. I love you, Katherine."

Katherine took a steadying breath. Her insides trembled with anxiety. "You say it doesn't matter, but what happens a year from now?" She looked into his eyes, all the fear and panic that churned inside her making her tremble. "What about five years from now, Scott? What happens then?"

"As long as we love each other, everything else can be managed, and I know for a fact there's nothing that can outweigh the love I feel for you."

"I've watched you, watched you at the press conference and at the auction. It was very obvious how uncomfortable you felt being in the spotlight. What happens when…" Panic rose up inside her almost to the point of choking off her words entirely. "What happens when someone calls you Mr. Fairchild rather than referring to me as Mrs. Blake? Will you be able to manage that?"

"You're scaring me. What are you trying to say?"

"I'm only trying to bring the obvious problems out in the open, problems that will be very real, problems that will be unique to our situation. It's not a matter of money. We both come from wealthy families, but I seem to spend so much time in the glare of newspapers and social media while you've been able to maintain a low profile."

He wrapped his arms tightly around her. "I love you more than I'm capable of telling you. I know there will be problems we'll have to overcome, problems unique to our special situation that we'll need to face honestly and openly. We can work them out together. Our love will allow us to handle whatever comes along. Marry me, Katherine."

Her mouth was so close to his that their lips

brushed together as she whispered, "What about Jenny?"

****

George Weddington unrolled the plans on top of the table in Scott's office. "I've incorporated all the changes you asked for. Does this look like what you had in mind?"

Scott studied the blueprints, noting the changes from the original plans. "The more I think about it, the more I feel we should extend this wall out another five feet and add the other room we discussed. If we put it here—" He indicated the place on the blueprints. "—we can do it without disturbing that large old oak tree."

George sighed as he rolled up the plans. "If you don't stop changing things, you'll never be able to start construction. I can see it now. We'll be into the next decade, and you'll still be moving walls and changing windows." He gave Scott a warm smile. "I'll make the changes this afternoon."

"I promise, this will be it—honest."

The two men shook hands, and George left Scott's office.

Scott leaned back in his chair and swiveled around until he could look out the window. The past two weeks had been the busiest of his life. Too many projects and too little time. The weather had been unseasonably warm and dry. Hopefully, it would hold a while longer. He didn't want bad weather to delay completion of his primary construction project.

He glanced at his watch. He needed to be on his way. He had a meeting at the attorney's office, then that most important of meetings immediately afterward, a meeting with the state's child welfare agency.

****

Snow blanketed the surrounding mountains with a pristine cover of soft white, accentuating the brilliant blue waters of Lake Tahoe. The branches of the pine trees drooped low as the clumps of snow adhered to the pine needles. Large wet flakes floated by the windows as they gently fell from the skies. The scene looked as though it had been taken directly off the front of a Christmas card. A roaring fire danced and crackled in the large stone fireplace. Two pairs of skis and two sets of ski poles rested in the corner with two pairs of ski boots on the floor next to them.

Scott filled Katherine's cup with hot, spiced cider, laced with a noticeable amount of brandy, then filled his own cup. They sat on the floor, warming themselves in front of the fire. He leaned close to her, brushed his lips against hers. "Are you sure you don't want me to try for some dinner reservations for tonight?"

Her laugh was soft as she stroked his cheek with her fingertips and returned his tender kiss. "You can't wait until the afternoon of December 31st to start thinking about dinner reservations for New Year's Eve. Besides, I'd rather spend the evening away from all those crowds of people." She snuggled in his arms. "I'd rather spend the evening right here, just the two of us."

He kissed her cheek. "Me, too." He furrowed his brow in thought for a moment. "How long can we stay here? I mean, just the two of us before some of your family shows up?"

"Day after tomorrow Uncle Charlie and Aunt Rose will be here. By the end of the week, their whole family will be here including grandkids and great-grandkids."

"Ouch! Then we need to be out of here after New

Year's Day or be inundated with your relatives."

She laughed at the scrunched-up expression on his face. "That's not polite, but it's definitely accurate."

He turned her around in his arms until she faced him. His gaze moved over her face, then settled on her eyes. "I love you so much. You're my life, my reason for being." He lowered his head to hers, capturing her mouth in a loving kiss.

She returned his kiss, conveying all the deep feelings she held for him. "I never knew it was possible to love someone as much as I love you."

He cupped her face in his hands, his expression very serious. "I know we discussed it, and I know I agreed with you, but I can't wait any longer." He rose to his feet, pulling her up with him. "Right now!"

"Now?"

"Yes, right now." He pulled her along behind him as he walked across the room. They drove directly to their intended destination. And finally the fruition of their quest.

"Do you, Katherine Sutton Fairchild, take this man…"

Scott clasped her hand tightly in his as the ceremony began. The small wedding chapel, located at the water's edge on the Nevada side of the lake, was only a few blocks from the Fairchild family lodge.

They had discussed the wedding several times. Neither wanted a large society wedding. Besides, as Katherine pointed out to Scott, it was her second marriage. A large, formal wedding seemed inappropriate. He had questioned her carefully, wanting to satisfy himself that she was not just saying that because all the publicity would make him uncomfortable.

She finally convinced him that she did not want to be married on the society pages of the newspaper any more than he did. They had decided on a small, private ceremony on Valentine's Day. The house Scott was having built would be ready by then. They had both immediately fallen in love with the large lot in Mill Valley, across the Golden Gate Bridge from San Francisco in Marin County. It was in a quiet neighborhood of stately old oak trees. Scott had commissioned George Weddington to design the house and had started a construction crew working on it as soon as the plans were ready.

"Do you, Scott Justin Blake, take this woman..."

Even though they had agreed on a small intimate ceremony, neither had ever dreamed they would actually end up getting married on the spur of the moment on New Year's Eve while dressed in ski clothes. But as Scott had said, he could not wait any longer. After getting over her surprise, Katherine had agreed. And now, here they were standing in front of a Justice of the Peace exchanging their wedding vows.

Following the brief ceremony, they returned to the Fairchild family lodge.

Katherine lay in Scott's arms, nestled in the warmth of the king-size bed. He slowly and sensually stroked his fingertips along the length of her body. "This is it, the wedding night." He fixed her with a teasing grin. "Tell me, Mrs. Blake, are you prepared?"

She returned his teasing. "I think I'll be okay as long as you promise to be gentle with me."

He rolled her over on top of him and whispered in her ear, "I don't know, you get me so excited sometimes I lose all control." His hand slid seductively across the smooth roundness of her bare bottom.

His growing arousal pressed against her. In a voice rapidly becoming thick with passion, she murmured in his ear, "I guess I'll just have to take my chances."

Her mouth found his as they melted into the heat of their passions, fueled by their deep and intense love for each other. Their tongues twined, their hands caressed and explored, their bodies became one. They made love with all the passion yet all the tenderness each was capable of giving. Nothing existed at that moment beyond the deep and unconditional love they felt for each other. They finally fell into a blissful sleep, each totally satiated from a night of intense lovemaking.

****

The aroma of freshly brewed coffee slowly penetrated Katherine's sleep-fogged brain. She opened her eyes and reached for Scott but found herself alone in the large bed. She was about to get out of bed when he came through the door carrying a breakfast tray.

He smiled when he saw she was awake. "Good morning, sleepyhead. I was beginning to think you were going to spend the rest of your life in bed."

She grinned impishly at him. "I can think of far worse ways to spend the rest of my life." Her expression turned serious. "In fact, as long as you're with me, I can't think of a better way to spend the rest of my life."

Scott set the tray on the nightstand, then sat down next to her. "I can't think of anything I'd rather do. I love you, Mrs. Blake."

She reached out and caressed his cheek. "Mrs. Blake...I like the sound of that. I love you, too, Mr.

Blake."

"It's a beautiful day. The sun is shining, the snow is sparkling, and the air is crisp and clean. It's the first day of the year and—" He leaned forward and kissed her tenderly on the lips. "—the first day of our lives together."

Epilogue

The first day of July, on a warm summer morning, Scott carried a breakfast tray into the bedroom and set it in front of Katherine. "Happy six-month anniversary." He leaned forward and kissed her.

"Mommy...mommy..." Jenny burst into the room.

Scott caught her just in time to avoid the disaster of her knocking over the tray and spilling hot coffee all over the bed. "Look what Skippy did to my doll."

The little beagle puppy scampered into the room and tried to jump up on the bed. "No, you don't." Scott picked up the puppy, scratched him affectionately behind his floppy ears, then placed him on the floor. "Not on the bed."

Jenny held the doll up to Scott. "Can you fix her, Daddy? Please, Daddy?"

He took the doll and the arm that the puppy had chewed off. "Let's look at it and see what we can do." After a closer inspection, he realized that the doll's arm had actually been torn out of the socket rather than chewed in two. It could be repaired. "You know you can't leave your toys on the floor. Skippy is still a little puppy, and he likes to chew on things." He went over to the French doors leading to the terrace and opened them, letting in the fresh air. "Why don't you and Skippy go play in the yard?"

"Come on, Skippy." Jenny ran outside with the puppy scampering after her.

"Look at her, Scott. Isn't it wonderful? She's finally able to be a happy little girl—a backyard with a swing and a little puppy to tag along after her. It's just the way I dreamed it would be. She hasn't had a single nightmare in months. It's almost as if they ceased the moment the ink dried on the adoption papers."

"I was beginning to think we'd never get through all the red tape. I had no idea adoption was such a lengthy process. We started all this the first of November, and it was the first of February before everything was finalized." He sat down on the bed next to her, enfolding her in his warm embrace. "I thought adoption was supposed to be quick, instant family as opposed to the good old-fashioned way."

He tickled his fingers across her abdomen and kissed her cheek. "This little fellow—"

"Hold on, there. It was only yesterday that the doctor confirmed I was pregnant. We don't know that it's going to be a boy. Maybe it will be a little girl."

"It has to be a boy"—he shot her a mischievous grin—"otherwise I'll be badly outnumbered. The only man in a house full of women."

Katherine tried to give him a stern, serious look. "Don't be ridiculous. Skippy is a male."

He held her in his arms and brushed his lips lightly against her cheek as they watched Jenny and the puppy playing in the yard. "What kind of a name is Skippy for a dog? When he grows up, all the other dogs will tease him."

"You know it's the only name Jenny wanted from the moment she laid eyes on him."

Scott sighed as he repeated Katherine's words, more to himself than anyone else. " 'Skippy is a male.' It's not quite the same, my love. It's not quite the same thing."

A word about the author…

I've lived most of my life in Los Angeles and earned my living for twenty years by working in television production. I was always interested in writing and dabbled at it, but not seriously. I combined my interest in writing with my avocation of photography and began doing magazine articles featuring my photographs. After selling several articles, I discovered I enjoyed the writing process as much as the photography.

My friends told me I should make use of my television contacts and write scripts. I enrolled in a screen writing class at UCLA. By the close of class, I knew screenwriting was not for me. The other thing I knew was that I wanted to write novels rather than magazine articles.

~*~

Visit Shawna at

www.shawnadelacorte.com